CHASING
THE SUN

CHASING THE SUN

Stories from Africa
Edited by Véronique Tadjo

A & C Black • London

To Nick, Larry and Matteo
for your inspiration and support

First published 2006 by
A & C Black
an imprint of Bloomsbury Publishing Plc
50 Bedford Square, London, WC1B 3DP
29 Earlsfort Terrace, Dublin 2, Ireland

www.bloomsbury.com

Collection copyright © 2006 Véronique Tadjo
Illustrations copyright © 2006 Véronique Tadjo
page 144 constitutes an extension of this copyright page

The right of Véronique Tadjo to be identified as the
illustrator of this work has been asserted by her in accordance
with the Copyrights, Designs and Patents Act 1988.

ISBN 978-0-7136-8217-5

A CIP catalogue for this book is available from the British Library.

Printed and bound by CPI Group
(UK) Ltd, Croydon, CR0 4YY

7 9 10 8

Contents

Contents

Introduction
by Véronique Tadjo

Traditionally, folk tales from Africa were told in local languages by storytellers who were also gifted musicians, poets and performers. The storytelling sessions usually took place in the open air, at home or during public gatherings. Very often, a tale would be told to all the members of the village but how it was understood differed depending on the age, gender and education of the listeners.

With the introduction of Western education during the colonisation of Africa in the 19th century, many of the ancient oral stories were translated into European languages like English, French and Portuguese. Then they were compiled into book form to make them accessible to a wider public.

Of course, African literature has changed tremendously with time, but it is fitting that the first stories in this collection, like 'Sun, Wind and

7

Cloud', are written in the oral tradition style. In 'Leuk-the-Hare Discovers Man', animals act like humans, taking on their vices and virtues, while 'Why the Mosquito Lives in the Bush' provides an explanation for life, and answers questions about the balance between man, animals and the environment. It gives a humorous interpretation of the way nature came to be what it is. 'The Drum' is also inspired by oral tradition and puts the good of society above individual interest.

Other stories show a new type of writing, in which the oral tradition is less obvious. They are created especially for the young readers of today. 'A Lion Hunt' is about growing up, coming of age and understanding life and its challenges. And 'Sosu's Call' deals with the difficult subject of disability. In 'The Little Blue Boy' it is the young hero's fight against prejudice and rejection that gives the story a universal appeal.

The clash that occurred when colonial powers like Great Britain, France and Belgium imposed their way of life on Africans was a recurrent theme in African literature at one point. The characters in the stories were caught in the turmoil of difficult cultural changes and oppression.

However, since they acquired independence from the West, many African countries have struggled to achieve democracy and real economic progress. Consequently, people become disillusioned and writers began to be critical of their own regimes. 'Half a Day', for example, mixes fantasy with realism to show that cities have grown uncontrollably and that they are now unpleasant to live in. In 'Bulubulu and Bamboko' the author uses humour and satire to make his point. He successfully shows the social and economic injustices in his country using two families of rats. It is funny, but also very moving.

Of course, hope is still present. In 'Miss Johnson', the readers are shown the redeeming power of art and beauty and the value of human relationships. Despite her modest life, the main character manages to find happiness while changing other people's lives, too. And although 'Citronella' has a sad ending, it is in fact full of hope for the future because it shows the importance of learning to listen to your inner self and of being in tune with the environment. Before passing away, the grandfather gives Citronella some of his knowledge and wisdom. The final story, 'Father, Who Are You?' is about learning to accept who you are and preparing for the future even though the present might be difficult.

The stories in this collection touch on a wide range of topics that illustrate the changing face of

Africa. You'll find that they can be funny or sad, instructive or simply entertaining to read. And there are many more out there. Once you've read these, why don't you continue the chase for the sunny side of life...

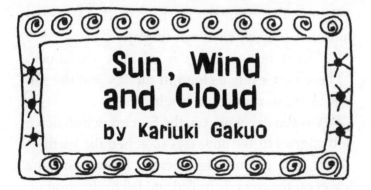

Sun, Wind and Cloud
by Kariuki Gakuo

A long, long time ago the Sun and the Wind had a quarrel. They could not agree which was the stronger.

"I'm stronger than you," said the Sun. "If I get angry, the whole world will dry up from the heat of my rays."

"Oh no, you're not," replied the Wind. "When I get angry, even the mountains tremble with fear."

A small, white Cloud was floating overhead. She heard the argument between the Sun and the Wind, and stopped to listen.

"Which one of us is stronger?" asked the Sun and the Wind together.

"Well," said the little Cloud, "there's only one way to find out. I suggest you have a competition."

"Then I will start," said the Sun, "for I know I shall win."

The Sun smiled golden and bright and spread his beams into the most distant corners of the world.

When the animals of the world saw the sunshine, they all went out to play.

"What a beautiful day it is," they exclaimed. "There isn't a single cloud in the sky and the sun is looking so round and bright."

But as the day wore on, the Sun grew hot, fierce and angry. His burning rays scorched the earth.

The soft, green grass became brown and the leaves on the trees shrivelled and fell to the ground.

All the rivers dried up and not a single drop of water could be found.

The animals were alarmed. "Ngai, the god of all living things, is angry. What shall we do?" they asked each other.

Mzee Kobe, the ancient tortoise, was the oldest and wisest animal on earth. The animals went to seek his advice.

"We are afraid that Ngai is angry with us. What shall we do?" they asked.

Mzee Kobe peered into the sky through his cloudy spectacles. He shook his head, wiped his glasses and peered again at the bright blue sky.

"We have done wrong. We must send a messenger to Ngai and beg for rain. Who shall be chosen for this important task?"

All the animals were eager to go. Above the chatter came a loud roar that made the hills and the mountains tremble.

"I shall go," roared the lion.

"No, no, no," Mzee Kobe shook his head. "Your voice is far too loud. You might anger Ngai further with your mighty roar and then he will not send us rain."

"Then I shall go," said the crested crane, strutting proudly. "Look at my golden crest. It is much more beautiful than the lion's mane. Ngai will listen to me."

The crested crane ruffled her feathers and the sun shone on the golden crown. All the animals gasped in admiration.

"No, no, no," Mzee Kobe shook his head again. "Ngai does not like animals who are proud and vain. Who else will go for us?" he asked.

The tiny dik-dik stepped forward. "I will go. I am as swift as an arrow. I can be there by evening."

Mzee Kobe peered at the dik-dik through his cloudy spectacles and nodded.

"You are small, humble and swift. You will make a fine messenger. Go now to Ngai's resting place on top of Mount Kirinyaga."

All the animals cheered and clapped as the tiny dik-dik sped away, as fast as a hunter's arrow.

The Sun and the Wind watched the dik-dik as he dashed away.

"There you are," said the Sun. "I am so strong that the animals have been forced to ask Ngai for help. Now it is your turn to show your strength."

The Wind was very clever. She saw a hut in the middle of the forest. Inside the hut a fire was burning brightly.

Blowing hard through the cracks in the walls, the mighty Wind lifted up a glowing red coal from the fire and let it fall onto the dry, brown grass outside. The grass began to burn, sending wisps of smoke into the blue sky.

Blowing even harder, the roaring Wind made the trees shake and the animals shiver. The fire began to spread. It spread from the grass to the bushes and then to the tall trees. As the Wind blew harder and harder, so the fire spread further and further.

A tall giraffe looked across the thorny acacia and saw the hungry flames licking at the dry trees.

"Run, run," she screamed, "the whole world is on fire!"

Kicking up her heels, she fled for her life, her long neck bobbing up and down over the blazing treetops.

"Run, run," growled the cheetahs as they sprang into the air and raced off away from the flames.

Gazelles, hyenas, kudus, jackals all followed, racing madly away from the crackling fire.

Monkeys screamed as they swung from tree to tree, the sparks of the fire landing on their coats, adding more frenzy to their escape.

The hooves of the animals made a noise like a thousand drummers which could be heard for many miles.

The Wind huffed and puffed until the whole sky became a blazing red and orange.

"Stop, stop!" shouted the Sun.

But the proud Wind would not listen. She wanted to show the world that she was the strongest of all. She blew harder until the thick, black smoke covered the little Cloud, filling her eyes with tears.

"Stop, stop!" coughed the little Cloud, but the Wind would not listen.

The little white Cloud grew thick and heavy from the black smoke. Soon her eyes became so sore that she began to cry. The rain fell down in torrents.

Lightning flashed through the sky and claps of booming thunder made the earth tremble.

When the animals heard the thunder, they stopped their flight and looked up into the sky.

"Ngai has answered our prayers!" they said as they danced with joy in the heavy rain and began to sing their rain song:

"Open your wings, your wings,
We'll fly to the sky,
Then the sky will cry,
And the rain will fall,
And put out the fire,
And the grass will grow,
And feed the calves."

The sound of their singing reached the little Cloud, and she was so happy that she cried even harder. As the rain reached the ground it began to put out the fires.

More rain fell and the rivers began to flow again. The dry earth soaked up the falling rain and new grass grew, covering the land with a sparkling green.

Trees swayed with joy to feel new leaves covering their bare branches and the animals relaxed, wandering peacefully on the grassy plains and drinking from the flowing rivers.

In the sky, Sun and Wind agreed that Cloud was stronger than either of them.

Even to this day, when the animals see the clouds growing dark and heavy with rain, they stop what they are doing to give thanks and praise to Ngai, the god of all living things, who saved them from both drought and fire.

Leuk-the-Hare Discovers Man
by Léopold Sédar Senghor

Back from his trip to the sea, Leuk is resting for a few days. The long journey has exhausted him. But he won't stay long in bed. Now, his greatest wish is to meet Man.

Once his strength is back, he starts preparing for a new trip. It will lead him to Nit-the-Man who lives in open-air spaces, far away from animals, out of the bush and the forest.

Leuk remembers the words of Diargogne-the-Spider, who told him: "You will get to know Man. He is a dangerous animal."

One fine morning, Leuk sets off. While on his journey, he notices the changes in the way the land looks. He discovers big, fenced-off fields and hedges. Everywhere, he notices a network of paths. They bear the marks of footsteps he has never seen.

The first man he glimpses is a herdsman whose cattle wander around. As soon as he sees him, Leuk stops to watch from a distance.

The man carries a long stick across his shoulders. He moves here and there and sings all the time. Occasionally, he shouts something at the animals. They then huddle together.

"Diargogne-the-Spider is right," thinks Leuk. "This animal must be very dangerous because just with his voice, he can control beasts much bigger than him."

Leuk notices another animal who looks very much like those of the bush. He runs up and down yelling at the cattle.

"He must be Man's assistant," Leuk says to himself. "He, too, is certainly as dangerous as his master."

But Leuk wants to know more about Man. He wants to see him from close up to know how he lives, speaks and takes care of his family. In order to do this, he has to go further into the built-up area etched against the sky.

As he advances, the outline of the pointed huts which make up the village becomes clearer and taller. It looks like the whole village is running to meet him.

From this village, different noises rise up in the air: people calling loudly, bursts of laughter, pounding, hammering and threshing. Leuk sees some men and women who are coming and going, children who are playing, falling, getting up and gesticulating like little devils.

Drawing nearer, he reaches the dump on which the villagers throw their rubbish. On the dump, he sees many farm animals: hens, guinea fowls, ducks, dogs, cats, and so on. While some scratch and peck about, others forage with their muzzle, and roll over in the dust.

When they see Leuk, all of them raise themselves up, surprised, wide-eyed, and with straight necks.

"Good morning, my friends!" says Leuk, the visitor from the bush, kindly.

Then the hens start to cackle, the ducks start quacking, the dogs start howling and the goats start bleating out of fright.

Made unhappy by this welcome, Leuk goes away as fast as he can and enters the yard of the first house he finds.

In the yard, he meets two children who are playing with some earth and some stones. The kids have never seen a hare. Nevertheless, they are not afraid. Leuk seems kind and cute in their eyes.

"Come closer," they tell him. "You look friendly. Allow us to stroke you a little."

Leuk is happy to draw near and the children run their small hands over his smooth fur.

"He feels like a lamb," says one.

"He looks more like a kitten," says the other.

Towards the end of the day, as the sun is coming down, the father of the two children returns from his fields.

"Father, we have made a new friend!" they shout happily.

"A new friend?" asks the father, not really believing them. He goes to them. As soon as he sees Leuk, he stops in his tracks.

"What? This is what you call your new friend?" he says laughing. You should know, my dear children, that you are dealing with the most cunning of all the animals of the bush. You must beware of him as he is capable of playing nasty tricks on you."

"For a start," adds the father, "I am going to lock him up in the cubby-hole where we keep our harvests. He will feed himself well there and will grow fatter. Afterwards, we will talk about him again."

Upon hearing about this, all the members of the family come with mocking eyes to have a look at Leuk. So, the two children start to cry as though their hearts would break.

In the dark cubby-hole where he is locked up, Leuk thinks long and hard about his lack of caution. The words of Diargogne-the-Spider come back to him. Here he is, a prisoner of Man who will probably roast and eat him.

Leuk spends the whole night sleepless. He thinks that he will never again see his beautiful forest, the quiet savannah and his friends, the animals.

The next day, one of the children comes to him.

"I want to save you, my friend," the child says.

"How will you be able to save me?" asks Leuk.

"Give me your ears through these two wooden poles and be courageous."

Leuk does as he is told. The child pulls Leuk's ears with all his might. In one vigorous move, he wrings him out of the confined space.

As fast as an arrow, Leuk rushes towards the fields. But all the dogs of the house are released and sent after him. Just as he is about to disappear into a thick bush, one of the dogs gets hold of his tail and *chomp!* nearly bites it off.

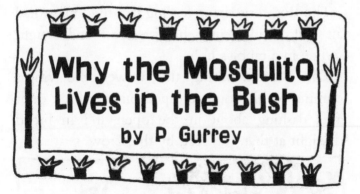

Why the Mosquito Lives in the Bush
by P Gurrey

One evening the Mosquito, giving the Iguana an account of the yam harvest he had dug with his father that day, said: "Dear Iguana, we dug up some enormous yams in our farm today. One yam my father dug up was so big that it was just about as big as my leg!"

The Iguana looked a bit blank and then asked him to repeat his story. When he had told it again, and said the yam was so big that it was as big as his leg, the Iguana said grumpily: "I would rather choose to be deaf than to hear such incredible stories. What is the Mosquito's leg compared to any yam worthy of the name?" So he stuffed his ears with two sticks.

Next morning when the Boa constrictor met the Iguana, he politely greeted him, but his old friend did not turn to greet him and made no reply; he just looked straight ahead and was indifferent to the pleasant greeting.

The Boa constrictor, fearing that the Iguana had an evil mind against him, ran off and sought refuge in a rabbit's hole.

The Rabbit, seeing this unwelcome visitor coming to his house, escaped out the back door and, dashing about in the open and in broad daylight at that, was seen by the Crow.

As seeing a rabbit in daytime was regarded as a sign that something dreadful was about to happen, the Crow raised an alarm and cawed for help.

The Monkey, answering the alarm call, and jumping from tree to tree to help, landed on a dead branch which broke, so that he fell onto the nest of the Owl, and killed one of his young ones.

When the Mother Owl returned from her breakfast and found her nestlings crying, she said: "Stop screeching and tell me what is that matter."

So when they told her she began to mourn for her nestling and refused to 'hoot' in order to let the next day break, for that was her duty as she was always awake at night.

As the night was already unusually long, the other animals sent a delegation to the Owl to enquire why she had not 'hooted' so that the day could break.

She said she was mourning her dead nestling that the Monkey had killed.

So the Monkey was called upon to account for the murder. He defended himself by saying: "I was hastening to help the Crow, who had raised an alarm and, as the branch broke, it was an accident."

So they asked the Crow: "Why did you raise an alarm?"

"Because I saw a rabbit running around in the daytime. Wasn't that sufficiently alarming?"

So then they asked the Rabbit: "Why break a law of nature, Rabbit, and run about in the daytime?"

"Because the Boa constrictor entered my house, and I ran for my life, too frightened to know where to go," he answered.

"And what were you doing in Rabbit's house, you long thing?" they asked the snake.

"I feared that my old friend, the Iguana, whom I greeted this morning, and who would not answer, intended some evil against me."

The Iguana, of course, could not hear when they called him to come to explain the case; but they soon discovered the two sticks poking out of his ears. So they removed the sticks, and then he told them the fantastic story of the Mosquito's large yams, which had made him decide never to hear again.

Mosquito meanwhile had heard the buzz of the enquiries finishing up with the Iguana, and so knew that he would be called to judgement. He then begged the Wind to help him.

"Mosquito," called the animals all together, "you are the cause of the unfortunate death of the Nestling Owl which has led to this never-ending night! Come and defend yourself!"

"Yes, yes, yes," he sang out, "I'm coming, yessssssssss," but they could only hear a buzz, for Wind had come and blown him away into the bush.

Now that is why the Mosquito lives in the bush; but when at night he enters the house, and whispers into people's ears, he is asking: "How has my case been decided? Am I condemned?"

The Drum
by Chinua Achebe

Long, long ago, when the world was young, all the animals lived together in one country. In those days there were not as many tortoises as there are today but only one tortoise, Mbe, the ancestor of all the tortoises and his wife, Anum. Similarly, there was Anunu, the father of all birds, there was Ebunu, the ram and his wife, Atulu; Enyi, the elephant; Agu, the leopard; Odum, the lion and many others.

For many years all of these animals lived a happy life. The winds blew and the rains fell in their season and the crops grew and there was enough for everyone to eat and drink.

But one year the rain began to fail, the sun came out more than usual and the dry season stretched far into the months that belonged to rain. The following year was much the same, and the year after that was even worse. The soil became so hot and dusty that seeds could no longer stay alive in it, let alone grow. The rivers and streams began to dry up. Drought had descended on the world. And with drought came famine.

The animals who had always enjoyed three meals every day began to eat only twice a day, and then once. By the third year most of them were lucky if they found one meal in three days. There was great sorrow in all the land.

One day, Tortoise set out from home in the early morning in search of wild fruits and berries. By noon the sun was beating down on the earth without mercy and Tortoise, tired and sweating, had not found even one berry. As he trudged along the burning footpath, nothing stirred or made the slightest sound. And so Tortoise heard his own footsteps on the hot sand and they seemed to say:

Aja mbene
Mbe mbene
Aja mbene.

Then a tall palm tree came into view. Tortoise's heart began to beat faster as he padded slowly toward its shade. He looked up its long, heavy trunk to its head and asked if it had any ripe palm fruit. In those days trees and animals had one language and so understood one another. The palm tree replied that it had one ripe fruit. Though hungry and tired, Tortoise was angry and disappointed. One fruit! To climb that long and heavy trunk all the way into the clouds for one palm fruit! Tortoise also knew too well how palm fruits were surrounded by hard and sharp thorns. He knew how firm they could be and how difficult it was to pull them out before they were fully ripe. And there was yet another problem – how to know which of the hundreds of fruits in the bunch was the ripe one. Or should he simply go from one fruit to the next ... and the next ... bruising his fingers in the thorns until he chanced on the lone ripe fruit? Oh no! No Tortoise would do that kind of stupid thing! And what if he should fall down from the terrible height while he was searching the foolish bunch from thorn to thorn? Tortoise became truly angry with the tree and particularly with the land on which it grew. He cursed the hopeless and wretched soil, the tired and exhausted soil, the stupid soil that could do no better than a palm tree with one ripe fruit at its head! And he moved on. His anger seemed to have put a new strength into his walk. But very soon he slowed down again and then felt even more tired than before. The sands grew hotter under his feet. And the sound of his tired walk became louder and louder in his head:

Aja mbene!
Mbe mbene!
Aja mbene!

In due course he came to another tree and asked how many ripe fruits it had.

"Three," replied the tree.

"Stupid land," cursed Tortoise. "Good-for-nothing useless land. Land that's only fit for Anunu, the bird, to dance upon. Shame! Four hundred times shame, on you!"

The next tree had ten fruits. Tortoise considered it for a while. Ten out of all those hundreds. It was still not worth it. What if he should miss his hold and fall from that great height? For ten tiny palm fruits. "Miserly land," he said, but he said it quietly under his breath. "Who knows, I may yet climb it if nothing better turns up," he thought.

But something much better did turn up: a moderately tall tree with thrice four hundred fruits!

"How many did you say, good tree?" asked Tortoise wondering if he had heard right.

"Thrice four hundred," replied the tree.

Tortoise danced a little way up the road and then back again. He thought he heard faint sounds of a drum rising from this good and generous earth. Or perhaps it was only happiness beating the drum in his heart. Thrice four hundred! One thousand and two hundred fruits!

He began to climb. His energy had returned to him. Even the sun now seemed to beat the earth less harshly. Half-way up the tree Tortoise felt a mild and pleasant wind begin to blow and cool him. He could now see the bunch clearly, with its thrice four hundred ripe fruits. Could he eat them all today or come back tomorrow? What if somebody else should come this way and discover the remnant of his banquet? Somebody like Anunu, the bird? No, it would be best to put everything in his stomach where it would be nice and safe. He chuckled aloud. "Thrice four hundred! A rather nice way of saying one thousand and two hundred."

He had now climbed to the neck of the palm tree right under the branch which supported the ripe bunch of fruits. He now climbed one step sideways and one step upwards and came level with the ripe fruits. He stretched his hand and pulled out the first fruit and threw it into his mouth. It was the best and sweetest palm fruit he had ever tasted. It was not very large but it was almost all flesh and no kernel. He picked another and another and another and crammed them into his mouth so that his cheeks bulged out on both sides. He chewed and chewed and swallowed the pleasant fresh juice and chewed and swallowed until all the juice was gone. Then he spat out the fibre and filled his mouth with five new fruits. Then he picked a sixth to hold in his hand. At the same time he tried to change his position on the tree slightly so as to get even closer to the fruits. In doing this the fruit slipped through his fingers and fell to the ground.

"I am sorry," said Tortoise, "but I will not allow even one of these marvelous fruits to get lost." And he began to climb down in search of the fallen fruit.

The fruit lay at the edge of a hole in the ground. "You see," said Tortoise to himself, "if I hadn't come down right away, some little animal living in this hole might have come up and taken my fruit."

As he stretched his hand to pick it up, it slid into the hole and lay just below the surface. Tortoise pushed in his hand to get it and it fell further in, just beyond reach but still quite visible. Tortoise noticed that the hole was really quite large and seemed to descend in steps.

"What is my name?" asked Tortoise of himself, "Am I not Tortoise who never gives up a fight half-way?"

He plunged into the hole and stretched out his arm to grasp his fruit. His fingertip just touched it and it fell further down onto the next step.

"Today is today," said Tortoise. "Wherever you go, my little fruit, Tortoise goes with you."

With the fruit always a little ahead of him, Tortoise descended deeper and deeper into the earth. Then all of a sudden he emerged out of a hole and found himself in a big clearing. There were huts and trees and farms. But the light was strangely mild and gave everything a tinge of yellow. Tortoise found a little boy standing close by, chewing something in his mouth.

"What are you chewing?" asked Tortoise.

"I am chewing a palm fruit," replied the boy. He spoke through his nose as if he had a head cold.

"Where did you find it?" asked Tortoise.

"I was sweeping our yard and it fell right here, out of the sky."

"I see," said Tortoise. "I suppose I too fell out of the sky?"

"Yes, sir," said the boy.

"Well, I didn't. And I have more news for you. I am Tortoise, the owner of the fruit you have just eaten."

"I am sorry, sir."

"No need to be sorry, my boy. Just find my fruit right now or I am taking you away to my country."

The little boy began to cry and his parents and other spirits rushed out from the huts and asked what was the matter. They all spoke through their noses.

"Your boy ate my palm fruit and I have asked him to give it back to me or else…"

"And who are you, if we may ask?"

"I am Tortoise who never gives up a fight half-way."

"I believe I have heard of you. We are spirits and this is our town. You are welcome, Tortoise." He turned to the boy and asked, "Did you eat Tortoise's palm fruit?"

The boy said, "Yes," with tears in his eyes. "I didn't know it was his."

"This is a simple matter," said the spirit. "We have many palm trees here," he said to Tortoise, "and we shall give you ten fruits for the one you lost."

"Oh no," said Tortoise. "My own fruit or else your boy goes with me."

The boy screamed and wailed when he heard this.

"Quiet!" said his father, and then turned again to Tortoise. "All right, we shall give you a whole head of palm fruits for your single fruit."

"I don't want to be offensive but really you are wasting my time," replied Tortoise. "My fruit or the boy. Finish!"

At this the boy fled, screaming, into one of the huts.

"Stop!" shouted Tortoise, running after him.

"Come on, my friend," said the elderly spirit, barring his way, "don't scare the poor boy. We will give you something which is better than all the palm trees in the world."

"And what may that be?"

"A drum."

"A drum? Do I look like a drummer to you? Look here, my good friend, I have been very patient…"

"You have indeed," said the spirit, "and we like you for it. The drum I will give you is no ordinary drum. Take it from me and you will be glad you did."

"All right," said Tortoise, "I shall accept the drum, but only because of your gentle manner and good words. But tell your boy to be careful in future and not gobble up any palm fruit that drops out of the sky. Where's the drum?"

They brought a strange little drum and its drumstick. Tortoise hung the drum from his shoulder by its strap and was about to beat it. But the spirit quickly held his hand.

"Not here," he said, "beat it gently when you get back to the world. And if it doesn't surprise you, I'll be surprised!"

Tortoise said goodbye to the spirits and began to climb up to the world of white light.

At the foot of the palm tree he beat the spirit drum. The sound that came out of it was unlike the sound of any drum he had ever heard:

Kpam putu! kpam putu!
Igba nni n'ofe!
Gidi gada! gidi gada!
Aneli n'anu!

Immediately a table loaded with food was set before him. All the good foods he had ever eaten and those he had only dreamt of lay profusely around. Yam and cassava, rice and beans, millet, fish and meat stew, egusi and okra soup and pots of palm wine. Tortoise ate as he had never eaten in all his life and drank a whole pot of palm wine. When he finally rose to go, he could hardly walk. He took three or four unsteady steps and then remembered the palm tree that had brought him all this good fortune. He walked back to it and patted its trunk fondly and said "thank you" five or six times, and set out for home with his drum. After a few steps, he remembered the hole in the ground and went back and knelt down and whispered "thank you" seven times into it. Then he began the journey home, whistling happily all the way.

At first Tortoise thought he should keep the drum a secret from the animals. But after one week of feasting with his wife in the innermost room of their home, another thought came to him. "If I feed the animals at this time when they are all about to perish from hunger, they will honour my name and perhaps even make me their king. That would be really nice!"

The only problem with this idea was that he could not say how long the food in the drum would last. Although after one week it still showed no sign at all of diminishing, yet who knew what would happen if the whole country began to feed from it?

In the end, Tortoise could not resist the thought of becoming a popular hero among the animals and perhaps their king. And if the food in the magic drum should run out, why, he could always go back to the spirits for another drum. They must have stacks and stacks of them.

So the next day an invitation went out to all the animals in the country. The messenger was Anunu, the bird, and his message was to tell all the animals to assemble in Tortoise's compound tomorrow at lunch time.

"Tell them," said Tortoise importantly and mysteriously, "that I have a message for them from the land of the spirits."

"From the land of the spirits?" asked Anunu, greatly surprised.

"That's right," said Tortoise, "from the very land of the spirits. Tell that to every one of them, to every single animal in the kingdom."

"In the kingdom? What kingdom?" asked Anunu, more puzzled than ever.

"Oh dear, dear, dear! My thoughts are running away with me this morning," said Tortoise. "No, my good friend, it was a slip of the tongue, as the saying goes. I did not mean to say *kingdom* but *country*. All the animals in the country. Here at my palace, I mean place. Lunch time tomorrow. Business: a very important message from spirit-land. Now, run along, my dear friend and I'll see you all tomorrow."

As he flew away, Anunu thought how very odd Tortoise was becoming these days.

"I hope he is not opening his old bag of tricks again," he said. "I wouldn't want to be part of it... Perhaps I should ignore his message and just fly home to my nest and endure my hunger in peace."

But there was something about Tortoise's manner which had convinced Anunu that he was serious. What was even more striking was the appearance of Tortoise and his wife. They seemed so well fed. And a man who looked so well at this time deserved to be listened to even if he was known to be something of a crook. So Anunu took Tortoise's message to all the animals in the country. Few animals honoured Tortoise's invitation. Some of the others thought it must be one of his practical jokes and stayed at home. A few were even angry. They thought that the very mention of lunch time at this time of general starvation was a cruel joke. And some were too weak and hungry to give any thought to the matter.

The few who came took their seats under the shade of a ragged old tree in Tortoise's compound. Monkey was there out of curiosity; Lizard came because his compound was just next door; Leopard was there determined to thrash Tortoise if the invitation should prove to be a hoax. And there were a handful of others who had one odd reason or another for coming.

When it became clear that no newcomers were expected, Tortoise rose to speak. He began with a well-known proverb: *If you underrate the little pot on the cooking stand, it will boil over and put out the fire.* "I know that I am only a tiny fellow compared to such giants as Elephant, Rhinoceros, Buffalo and the rest. And that, perhaps, is why so many have ignored my invitation. But little fellows sometimes have their uses."

"Please get to the point," growled Leopard.

"Oh I will, my dear Leopard, presently," said Tortoise, "but it is always wise to prepare the ground before sowing the seed. Our wise men have also told us that eating without asking questions causes dying without being sick."

"We have had enough jokes about eating from you," said Hedgehog, bristling with anger, "and I am getting quite impatient."

"All right, good people. Let me come to the point. The hunger in the land is something we all know about. We have all suffered from it for three years. And so, the other day, I said to myself: *All the animals in the country will perish unless somebody comes forward to save them. Somebody who is prepared to risk his own life for the sake of his fellows.* And so I decided that that person had to be myself…"

Some of the animals laughed at the thought. Tortoise as a saviour! What a joke.

"Go on, saviour," said Monkey.

"And so I said goodbye to my wife because I did not think I would return home alive," continued Tortoise. "And I did not tell her where I was going because I knew she would have tried to stop me."

"And where were you going, Crazy?" asked Goat.

"I was going to the land of spirits."

The animals roared with laughter. Goat is right, they thought. The fellow has gone crazy. Hunger has finally touched his brain. But Tortoise was now so overpowered by the story he was weaving that he did not even hear the mocking laughter.

"And so I journeyed for seven days and seven nights and crossed seven rivers and traversed seven grasslands. And finally I arrived in the land of the spirits and was taken to their king."

"Poor fellow," said Leopard, "his mind is gone." And he rose and left.

"To cut a long story short," said Tortoise, "I told the king of spirits that my people were dying of hunger in my country and I must find a cure or else die trying. The king then spoke. He said he had never seen a person who loved his people so much that he would brave the journey from the world of living creatures to the land of the spirits. He said his first thought had been to kill me. But my words and courage had changed his mind. So he called a big feast in my honour to which he invited all his noblemen and their ladies. And he made a long speech in my praise and ended it by giving me a chieftancy title. He called me Chief Tortoise Who Never Stops A Fight Half-Way."

The animals were no longer laughing or talking. Something in Tortoise's face and voice held their attention firmly.

"I could go on all afternoon telling you about the honours that the king heaped on me. But I shall reserve that story for another day. You must all be hungry and we should attend to that first."

The animals stared at one another in surprise.

"But before our feast I should tell you that the food you are going to eat comes from my brother and friend, the King of Spirits, to you my beloved people of the Kingdom – I mean to say the Country of Animals."

He turned round and walked slowly like a great chief to his hut. The animals sat in complete silence, watching. He soon returned carrying a strange drum from its strap on his left shoulder. He did not say another word when he got to his place before the little crowd. He just tapped the drum with the bent drumstick:

Kpam putu! kpam putu!
Igba nni n'ofe!
Gidi gada! gidi gada!
Aneli n'anu!

The way the animals went at the food was truly remarkable. They could have been starving for thirty years! Rat fell straight into the pot of egusi soup and was badly scalded, and Goat jumped with all four feet into the huge bowl of yams. Many of the dishes were overturned in the scramble and one or two were smashed all together and their contents were snatched greedily from the ground. But after a while the animals realised that there was enough food for the whole country to share peacefully. And so they settled down and gorged themselves without fighting.

The next day the whole country was at Tortoise's door at daybreak. He heard the tremendous noise of their presence and was happy. But he was not going to be rushed, he would do things at his own pace and in his own good time. He knew that that was the only way to make the animals accept his importance. A chief does not hurry. So Tortoise lay in bed listening to the hungry voice of the country and smiling contentedly.

After a very long while, the confused noise of the animals stopped and a chant like the roar of the ocean took its place:

WE! WANT! TOR! TOISE!
WE! WANT! TOR! TOISE!

Tortoise's heart was touched by this appeal. He got up from his bed, washed his face and hands and went out to meet his people.

WE! WANT! THE! DRUM!
WE! WANT! THE! DRUM!

"You will see the drum presently," said Tortoise, waving his hand to obtain silence. "You will see the drum, my good people. But first we must hear how the drum came into our hands. Those of you who answered my call yesterday already know the story. But there were only a handful of people. Today I am happy to see that we have the whole country. I want you all to hear the story as it happened, not as hearsay."

And he told the story of his self-sacrificing journey again. Those who had heard it yesterday noticed little differences here and there in today's telling. For instance Tortoise now said that when he told his wife he was going to the land of the spirits, she burst into tears. But nobody worried about such little details. The important thing was that he had gone to the land of the spirits on behalf of his people and bought home a priceless gift which was there for all to see.

Because of the much larger numbers present at the second feast, it was far rowdier than the first. Indeed it became a total riot. But again, as on the first day, some kind of order returned when the guests finally realised how large the feast was.

Every day, the animals returned to Tortoise's compound and ate and drank and went home singing his praise. They called him Saviour, Great Chief, the One Who Speaks For His People. Then one day a very drunken singer called him King Tortoise. Thereafter the great Chant of the Animals became:

WE! WANT! OUR! KING!!
WE! WANT! OUR! KING!!
OUR! KING! OF! KINGS!!

A day was set for the coronation. Silk robes were ordered from the Country of Insects and a crown from the Country of Fishes. Tortoise's compound was bedecked with flags and bunting. And Toad rehearsed the anthem he had composed with the Choir of State day and night.

Coronation morning! The day broke with a salute of twenty-one guns. The animals assembled for the pre-coronation breakfast. The toad and his choir rendered endlessly the new anthem: *OUR GREAT AND GLORIOSE KING TORTOISE.*

Tortoise decided that as king there were certain things he should no longer do, such as beating a drum. And so he appointed Elephant as his royal drummer. And thus it came about that on coronation morning as all the animals assembled for breakfast, Elephant picked up the magic drum for the first time and gave it a gentle tap with the drumstick. And such was Elephant's gentle tap that it ripped the hide from wood to wood! The little drum was broken!

And such was the cry that went up from the animals that King-elect Tortoise, who was not supposed to show himself to his people until the ceremonies at noon, rushed out in his loincloth. And he immediately saw the disaster. After the first shock, he took control of the situation. He sent two young animals to collect the latex of a certain tree and bring it to him. Meanwhile he made a short speech to his people and asked them to remain calm.

"This is only a temporary setback which we shall soon overcome," he said. "Our ceremony must proceed as planned. Nothing must shake us from our purpose."

The two animals returned with the latex and Tortoise applied it very skillfully to the broken membrane of the drum and put it in the sun to dry. The animals watched him in gloom and silence.

"Be of good cheer," said Tortoise to them, "everything will be all right, and we shall smile again."

The glue was now dry and the drum seemed in reasonably good shape. Tortoise picked it up under his arm and looked at the crowd of animals. They were so still, they seemed to be holding their breath. He tapped the drum with more care than he had ever shown. An indistinct whirring sound came out. Then a grain of rice dropped out; a crumb of yam and a strand of meat followed and then two drops of palm wine and a drop of egusi soup. The animals broke into a loud cry.

Tortoise made a short, moving speech to them in which he promised that as soon as his coronation was over he would return to his friend, the King of Spirits, to get another drum.

"Let us proceed with the ceremonies as planned."

But the crowd was beginning to break up. A voice was heard to ask: "Proceed on an empty stomach? Go and get the drum and then we shall proceed."

"Well spoken!" replied many voices. "The drum first and then the coronation. What's the good of a king without a food drum?"

And the animals began to leave Tortoise's compound in groups of three and four.

At the first crow of the cock, Tortoise was on his way to the land of spirits. By noon he was at the foot of the palm tree of thrice four hundred fruits.

"Good palm tree, do you have any ripe fruits?" he asked breathlessly. The tree said nothing. "I think you have something. Anyway I shall come up and see for myself," said Tortoise and began to climb. As soon as he got to the top of the tree, he picked one fruit and let it fall to the ground. Then he descended. The fruit had fallen a good distance from the hole in the ground. Tortoise rolled it gently with his foot towards the hole and then pushed it in. He knelt down and reached into the hole. And, to his annoyance, the fruit lay perfectly within his reach. He cursed it and then pushed it further down and then climbed in. Again it was within easy reach and again he called it a useless fruit and pushed it further and continued to curse and push all the way into the spirit land. The little spirit boy was standing by with his long broom, looking at the palm fruit when Tortoise jumped out of the hole. As soon as the boy saw him, he fled towards the huts.

"Don't run away from me, my little friend," said Tortoise in his gentlest voice. The boy stopped, turned around and gazed at Tortoise suspiciously.

"Don't be afraid of me, little fellow. I was only teasing you the other day. I enjoy teasing children: but I mean no harm. I am actually a great lover of children, as you will see when you come to know me better... I hope your parents are home because I have come specially to thank them for that marvellous little drum. My people were so happy with it that they made me their king. And so I have come back to thank your father. Is he home?"

"Yes, sir," said the boy. "He is in the hut. Shall I call him?"

"Don't worry," said Tortoise. "I shall walk over with you. But before I forget, I did bring a little present for you. I know you like palm fruits and so I brought you the sweetest fruit in the whole wide world. It dropped from my hand as I was coming down. Did you see it by any chance?"

"It's right there behind you."

"Of course it is. I'm getting old, you know, and my eyes are no longer what they used to be... Here we are. It's a little present from me to you."

The boy hesitated at first. But Tortoise, in his sweetest manner, persuaded him to accept the fruit.

"Come on," said Tortoise, "pop it in your mouth and tell me if it's not the sweetest palm fruit you ever tasted?"

The boy's eyes glowed as he munched the fruit. He was enjoying it so much that he didn't notice the change in Tortoise's face.

"Stupid boy. When will you ever learn? My fruit if you please!" shouted Tortoise, glaring ferociously at the boy and grabbing hold of his leg. The boy screamed in fear as he tried to break loose from Tortoise's iron grip.

"Oh no," said Tortoise, "you are going home with me this time without fail."

As before, the elders hearing the boy's cry, rushed out of their huts.

"I see," said the boy's father. "It's our old friend, Tortoise, playing with the boy."

"I am not playing, sir," said Tortoise stiffly.

"What's the matter, then?"

"In spite of my warning, you have not taught your boy to respect other people's palm fruits. That's what the matter is. And I have just told him that nothing – I repeat, nothing – will stop me from dragging him to my country by the ears."

"Please cool down, my good friend," said the spirit. "I am sure we can settle the matter more peacefully than that … what about … erm … another drum?"

Tortoise pretended to think about it for a while with his head thrown back and his head turned upwards.

"All right," he announced at long last. "But I want everybody to understand that this is the very last time I shall be persuaded to accept a drum for my flute – I mean to say, my fruit."

"We understand that perfectly well," said the spirit.

"Show me the drum!" said Tortoise in the tone of an emperor.

"This way, sir" said the spirit as he led the way to the back of one of the huts. It was just as Tortoise had imagined. There were scores of drums of various sizes hanging from wooden pegs driven into the mud wall.

"The choice is yours, sir," said the spirit with a wave of the arm towards the drums. Tortoise was overjoyed at the way things were turning out. The last time he was given a miserable little drum with a delicate skin. Now he had a chance to pick a drum befitting a king. So he marched up to the end of the hanging row of drums, looking at each as he passed, and finally pointing at the largest one of all.

"Fine," said the spirit, "that one it shall be. Will somebody get it down for our friend."

So Tortoise took the drum from one of the spirits and hung it on his shoulder. He picked up the curved drumstick, said farewell to the spirits and set out for home.

Tortoise was so pleased with himself that he whistled all the way up the seven great steps that led from the underworld. Out of the hole, at the foot of the palm tree, he paused to catch his breath. Then he realised that he was very hungry. He badly wanted to eat, but he also wanted to rush home and resume his interrupted coronation. He looked up at the sky for a time and found to his surprise that the sun was still overhead just as it had been when he went down the hole. Was it the same day or was it tomorrow or yesterday? He couldn't say. But whatever day, it was noon. So there was time to eat and also get home to his compound. He lifted the drum, which he had set down to rest his shoulder, and beat it gently. A strange and frightening noise issued from it — an ear-splitting scream followed by a short chant of hoarse male voices:

Pial'awo Pialu mbala!
Ufio!
Pial'awo Pialu mbala!
Ufio!

What happened next was even more frightening and strange. Masked spirits with bundles of whips appeared from nowhere and began rushing and jumping around and hitting at everything in their way. And they were soon followed by swarms of bees and wasps stinging away. Tortoise was so beaten and stung that he fell to the ground and passed out altogether and remained unconscious for a long time. When he opened his eyes again it was night. And he was so bruised and swollen that his shell could hardly contain him. "What happened? And where am I?" he wondered.

Slowly his memory began to come back to him, and with it a great fear. Where was the drum? And where were the masked spirits? Were they waiting in the darkness for him to wake up? Perhaps they were asleep and he should sneak away now before they woke up. But his effort to move caused him such sharp pains that he fainted again, and did not wake up until the afternoon of the next day.

When he came to, he took in the situation quietly with his eyes. The wicked drum lay innocently where he had dropped it. And heaps of broken whips lay scattered around. Everything else was normal: the palm tree of thrice four hundred fruits, a few ragged trees, a scorched countryside, a cloudless sky and a burning sun. Satisfied that there was no immediate danger, Tortoise stretched his limbs and found that he could just about manage to crawl home slowly and painfully. But there was really no reason to hurry now, he thought. He had more time than he could use. So he went back to sleep for another two days and took time to think things over and plan his future.

Tortoise's return to the Country of the Animals with the first drum had taken place at night. He had planned it that way so that no one would see him. But coming home now with the second drum, he chose the middle of the afternoon. As he walked slowly and deliberately towards his compound lugging the great drum, he was seen by many animals. Some of them went out happily to greet him and escort him home, while others rushed away to their friends to report the news. By evening, Tortoise's compound was full again and as noisy as usual. Very soon the chanting of the animals began:

WE! WANT! TOR! TOISE!!
WE! WANT! TOR! TOISE!!
WE! WANT! OUR! KING!!
OUR! KING! OF! KINGS!!

Tortoise, who had retired early to bed, got up again and went outside to speak to the animals. As soon as he emerged through the door of his hut, the animals sent up a deafening roar of applause. Tortoise held up his hand and there was immediate silence. He began to speak in a tired voice.

"My good people," he said. "I have made the journey as I promised you. And I have brought you a drum, a king of drums."

The animals clapped and cheered and jumped up and down. Tortoise held up his hand again.

"I had thought to rest tonight and present the drum to you in the morning…"

WE! WANT! IT! NOW!!
WE! WANT! IT! NOW!!
THE! KING! OF! DRUMS!!

"But I can see that you are impatient to see the drum," continued Tortoise, "and I can't say that I blame you. After all you have not tasted food for many days now. So I will present you the drum shortly."

There was a huge ovation when he said this. He held up his hand and then continued. "But I would be failing in my duty if I did not tell you something of the difficulties I had getting this drum. Some of you have already asked about the wounds all over my body. Well, my good people, you may remember I told you that it was no easy matter travelling to the land of the spirits. There are terrible monsters and demons along the way. I braved them all for your sake and took whatever punishment they gave. I shall say no more at present because I am very tired and must take my rest... But you may go ahead and have your dinner. I know I can trust you to conduct the dinner in an orderly fashion. In view of the accident we had with the last drum, I suggest that you appoint from among yourselves a new drummer with a lighter touch than our beloved Elephant."

This produced much laughter among the animals. Tortoise left them laughing and went back to his hut and returned with the large new drum. The animals cheered wildly.

"Enjoy yourselves," said Tortoise as he withdrew, waving. And he barred the door of his hut after him.

The animals elected Monkey as new State Drummer. But they did not want to offend Elephant too much so they made him State Trumpeter and Retired Drummer. Everyone was satisfied. Monkey came forward and lifted the drum to his shoulder. The animals gave him a loud cheer. He bowed to them in return. And then he picked up the drumstick with great dignity and tapped the drum.

When Tortoise barred the door to his hut, he did not retire to bed as he said he would. Instead he took his wife hurriedly out of the compound through a back exit deep into the bush behind his compound wall. His wife was surprised but Tortoise dragged her along. "This is no time to explain," he said to her. "Everything will be clear to you later." And so they went deeper into the bush until they came to a huge rock in a dry riverbed and took cover under it.

As for the animals, what they saw that evening has never been fully told. Suffice it to say that they dragged themselves out of Tortoise's compound howling and bleeding. They scattered in every direction of the world and have never yet stopped running.

A Lion Hunt
by Joseph Lemasolai Lekuton

My sweet mother,
Don't call me baby.
I stopped being a baby when I was initiated.

I'm going to tell you the lion story.

Where I live in northern Kenya, the lion is a symbol of bravery and pride. Lions have a special presence. If you kill a lion, you are respected by everyone. Other warriors even make up songs about how brave you are. So it is every warrior's dream to kill a lion at one point or another. Growing up, I had a lot of interaction with wild animals – elephants, rhinos, cape buffalo, hyenas. But at the time of this story – when I was about 14 – I'd never come face-to-face with a lion, ever. I'd heard stories from all the young warriors who told me: "Wow, you know yesterday we chased this lion—" bragging about it. And I always said "Big deal." What's the big deal about a lion?

It's just an animal. If I can defend myself against elephants or rhinos, I thought, why not a lion?

I was just back from school for vacation. It was December, and there was enough rain. It was green and beautiful everywhere. The cows were giving plenty of milk. In order to get them away from ticks, the cattle had been taken down to the lowlands. There's good grass there though it's drier than in the high country, with some rocks here and there. There are no ticks, so you don't have to worry about the health of the cattle, but the area is known for its fierce lions. They roam freely there, as if they own the land.

I spent two days in the village with my mum, then my brother Ngoliong came home to have his hair braided and asked me to go to the cattle camp along with an elder who was on his way there. I'd say the cattle camp was 18 to 24 miles away, depending on the route, through some rocky areas and a lot of shrubs. My spear was broken, so I left it at home. I carried a small stick and a small club. I wore my *nanga*, which is a red cloth, tied around my waist.

It took us all day to get there but at sunset we were walking through the gap in the acacia-branch fence that surrounded our camp. There were several cattle camps scattered over a five-mile radius. At night we could see fires in the distance, so we knew that we were not alone. As soon as we got there, my brother Lmatarion told us that two lions had been terrorising the camps. But lions are smart. Like thieves, they go somewhere, they look, they take, but they don't go back to the same place again.

Well, that was our unlucky day. That evening when the cows got back from grazing, we had a lot of milk to drink, so we were well fed. We sat together around the fire and sang songs – songs about our girlfriends, bravery songs. We swapped stories, and I told stories about school. The others were always curious to understand school. There were four families in the camp, but most of the older warriors were back at the village seeing their girlfriends and getting their hair braided. So there were only three experienced warriors who could fight a lion, plus the one elder who had come down with me. The rest of us were younger.

We went to bed around 11:30 or 12. We all slept out under the stars in the cattle camp – no bed, just a cowhide spread on bare soil. And at night it gets cold in those desert areas. For a cover I used the *nanga* that I had worn during the day. The piece of cloth barely covered my body, and I kept trying to make it longer and pull it close around me, but it wouldn't stretch. I curled myself underneath it trying to stay warm.

Everything was silent. The sky was clear. There was no sign of clouds. The fire was just out. The stars were like millions of diamonds in the sky. One by one, everybody fell asleep. Although I was tired, I was the last to sleep. I was so excited about taking the cows out the following morning.

During the middle of the night I woke to this huge sound – like rain, but not really like rain. I looked up. The starlight was gone, clouds were everywhere, and there was a drizzle falling. But that wasn't the sound. The sound was of all the cows starting to pee. All of them, in every direction. And that is the sign of a lion. A hyena doesn't make them do that. An elephant doesn't make them do that. A person doesn't. Only the lion. We knew right away a lion was about to attack us.

The other warriors started making a lot of noise, and I got up with them, but I couldn't find my shoes. I'd taken them off before I went to sleep, and now it was pitch black. Some warriors, when they know there's danger, sleep with their shoes in their hands and their spears right next to them. But I couldn't find my shoes, and I didn't even have a spear. Then the lion made just one noise: *bhwuuuu*! One huge roar. We started running towards the noise. Right then we heard a cow making a rasping, guttural sound, and we knew the lion had her by the throat.

Cows were everywhere. They ran into one another and into us, too. We could hear noises from all directions – people shouting, cows running – but we couldn't see a thing. My brother heard the lion right next to him and threw his spear. He missed the lion – and lucky for the rest of us, he missed us, too.

Eventually, we began to get used to the darkness, but it was still difficult to tell a lion from a cow. My brother was the first to arrive where the cow had been killed.

The way we figured it was this: two lions had attacked the camp. Lions are very intelligent. They had split up. One had stayed at the southern end of the camp where we were sleeping, while the other had gone to the northern end. The wind was blowing from south to north. The cows smelled the lion at the southern end and stampeded to the north – towards the other waiting lion.

When I asked my brother, "hey, what's going on? he said, "The lion killed Ngoneya." Ngoneya was my mother's favorite cow and Ngoneya's family was the best one in the herd. My mother depended on her to produce more milk than any other cow. She loved Ngoneya. At night she would get up to pet her.

I was very angry. I said, "I wish to see this lion right now. He's going to see a man he's never seen before."

Just as we were talking, a second death cry came from the other end of the camp. Again we ran, but as we got closer I told everyone to stop. "He's going to kill all the cows!" I told my brother. And I think this is where school thinking comes in. I told him, "Look, if we keep on chasing this lion, he's going to kill more and more. So why don't we let him eat what he has now, and tomorrow morning we will go hunting for him?"

My brother said, "Yes, that's a good idea," and it was agreed. For the first time I felt like I was part of the brotherhood of warriors. I had just made a decision I was proud of.

It was muddy, it was dark, we were in the middle of nowhere, and right then we had cows that were miles away. They had stampeded in every direction, and we could not protect them. So we came back to camp and made a big fire. I looked for my shoes and I found them. By that time I was bruised all over from cows banging into me, and my legs were bloody from the scratches I'd got from the acacia thorns. I hurt all over.

We started talking about how we were going to hunt the lion the next day. I could tell my brother was worried and wanted to get me out of danger.

He said, "Listen, you're fast, you can run. Run and tell the people at the other camps to come and help. We only have three real warriors here; the rest of you are younger."

"No way," I said. "Are you kidding me? I'm a warrior. I'm just as brave as you are, and I'm not going anywhere." At this point, I hadn't actually seen the lion, and I absolutely refused to leave.

My brother said, "I'm going to ask you one more time, please go. Go get help. Go to the other camp and tell the warriors that we've found the two lions that have been terrorising everyone, and we need to kill them today."

And I said, "No, I'm not going."

So he said, "Fine," and sent the youngest boy, who was only about eight.

When daylight came, I took the little boy's spear and walked out from the camp with the others. Barely two hundred yards away were the two lions. One had its head right in the cow, eating from the inside. And one was just lying around. She was full. As we approached them we sang a lion song: "We're going to get the lion, it's going to be a great day for all of us, all the warriors will be happy, we'll save all our cows."

As we got closer, the older man who was with us kept telling us to be careful. We should wait for help, he said. "This is dangerous. You have no idea what lions can do." But no one would listen to him.

The other guys were saying: "We can do it. Be brave, everyone." We were encouraging each other, hyping ourselves up.

My brother was so angry, so upset about our mother's favorite cow that he was crying. "You killed Ngoneya," he was saying. "You are going to pay for it."

Everyone was in a trance. I felt that something inside me was about to burst, that my heart was about to come out. I was ready. Then we came face-to-face with the lions. The female lion walked away but the male stayed. We formed a little semicircle around the male, with our long spears raised. We didn't move. The lion had stopped eating and was now looking at us. It felt like he was looking right at me. He was big, really big. His tail was thumping the ground.

He gave one loud roar to warn us. Everything shook. The ground where I was standing started to tremble. I could see right into his throat, that's how close we were. His mouth was huge and full of gore from the cow. I could count his teeth. His face and mane were red with blood. Blood was everywhere.

The lion slowly got up so he could show us his

full presence. He roared again. The second roar almost broke my eardrums. The lion was now pacing up and down, walking in small circles. He looked at our feet and then at our eyes. They say a lion can figure out who will be the first person to spear it.

I edged closer to my brother, being careful not to give any sign of lifting or throwing my spear, and I said, "Where's that other camp?"

My brother said to me, "Oh, you're going now?" He gave me a look – a look that seemed to say, you watch out because someone might think you are afraid.

But I said, "Just tell me where to go."

He told me.

I gave him my spear. "It will help you," I said, and then I took off in the direction of the other cattle camp. No warrior looked back to see where I was going. They were all concentrating on the lion.

As I ran toward the next camp, I saw that the little boy had done his job well. Warriors were coming, lots of them, chanting songs, asking our warriors to wait for them. The lion stood his ground until he saw so many men coming down, warriors in red cloths. It must have seemed to him that the whole hillside was red in colour. The lion then started to look for a way out.

The warriors reasoned that the lion had eaten too much to run fast and that the muddy ground would slow him up. They thought they could run after him and kill him. They were wrong. As soon as they took their positions, the lion surged forward and took off running. The warriors were left behind. There was nothing they could do except pray that they would meet this lion again.

From that time on, I knew the word in the village was that I had run away from the lion. There was no way I could prevent it.

"You know the young Lekuton warrior?"

"Yeah."

"He was afraid of the lion."

My brother tried to support me, but in our society, one word like that gets out, that's it. So I knew that I'd have to prove myself, to prove that I'm not a coward. So from then on, every time I came home on vacation, I went to the cattle camp on my own. I'd get my spear, I'd get my shoes. Even if it was 30 miles from the village, I'd go on my own, through thick and thin, through the forests and deserts. When I got there, I'd take the cattle out on my own. Always I hoped something would attack our cattle so I could protect them.

Sosu's Call
by Meshack Asare

Somewhere on a narrow strip of land between the sea and the lagoon, there is a small village. They say it was a bigger village. But with every crash of surf on the shore, the sea claims a sliver of the village. The lagoon stretches as far as the eye can see and it swells up whenever it pleases. But being the kind mother that the people believe it is, it drains out with just as much surprise.

That is why the people of the village are often heard to say: "The sea will only stop when the lagoon agrees to marry him."

Yet the people would not leave their village. The courtship between the sea and the lagoon is good for them, they say. The sea provides good fishing, while the lagoon supplies other delicacies. The soil too produces excellent vegetables for the market.

Sosu lives in the village with his parents, one sister, a younger brother, a dog and scores of chickens. Their house, like most other houses in the village, is only a stone's throw from the sea.

Most of the things he knows about the village are from the days when he was small enough to be carried around on his mother's back. That is a long time ago, when everyone fondly wished him to stand up on his legs and walk. But that did not happen.

So for many years, he only saw the world from inside the house. He saw the tall coconut palms waving their fronds in the breeze, high above the roofs. He saw the sky that seemed to end nowhere, the birds that floated free, the sun and the clouds.

In the mornings he sat by the door as everybody went away. Ma and Da were the first to go. Fafa and Bubu followed shortly as they went to school, with Fusa, their dog, running with them.

The dog was always back puffing, its eyes shining with the satisfaction of having been outside! And it was this, more than anything else, that made him envious. What good is a boy without a pair of good, strong legs?

Everyone cared for him. Da particularly did everything possible to make him feel like a normal boy. He taught him to repair broken fishing nets. Then he took him in his small canoe to paddle and fish in the lagoon. But one day while fishing with Da in the lagoon, two stern-looking men drew up alongside and said, "We don't think it wise to bring that boy of yours out here. It is unlucky enough to have the likes of him in the village. We doubt if the Lagoon Spirit is pleased to have him sitting here as well! We think you must keep him in your compound."

Then there was that awful night. The moon was a shiny pearl in the sky and everything was awash with its light! Even the tumbling sea had a silvery crest to its waves. So when the drums boomed and echoed, the message was clear: Come out to play! Come out! Come out to play!

Without thinking, Sosu dragged himself out of the compound. But while going towards the drumming in the moonlight, a girl appeared from nowhere and screamed so loudly that like flies to rotten fish, people came scurrying to the scene! Apparently she had taken him to be a creepy spirit!

This made him feel so miserable that even Fusa tried hard to cheer him up. Whenever he was by himself and quiet, the dog would insist that they play a game. Except even that did not help. All he did was throw a corn cob as far as he could. The dog then ran and leapt into the air to catch it before it touched the ground!

So, often, while the dog still hung in the air, feet,

tail and all, he would whistle for the chickens to come. He enjoyed watching them, perhaps because there was nothing to envy about them!

One thing he liked to do was get lunch ready for Fafa and Bubu, when they came home from school. It meant Ma having to set everything up for him. Often while they ate, they told him every new thing that they had learnt at school. That is how he too learnt to read and write, nearly as well as they did.

In the evenings, though, when everyone was home, it was a different matter. It seemed then that those with good legs should do everything. He could then very well be a newborn baby, or even a spirit that had to be served by others!

But one day, all of that changed. Well, nearly. It was a Monday, so everyone was away as usual. The men were out fishing, the women were hard at work on their gardens and the children were at school in the neighbouring village.

Everything looked all right. But suddenly, Fusa became restless and began to whimper and bark. The chickens too stopped scratching, jumped onto their perch on the rafters and remained still, except for their muted clucks and cackles.

Then a sudden darkness fell like a blanket across the sky! The usual, lazy yawn of the sea turned into an angry howl. The coconut leaves flapped and rustled as their tops bent and swayed desperately in the wind. And now the surf boomed and thundered as it crashed heavily against the sand!

As if that was not frightening enough, there was a loud bang! And with it, the old wooden gate shot across the yard like a massive kite. It only stopped after spinning and smashing into a wall, well away from everything.

Luckily, nobody was hurt and Sosu took a deep breath with relief. But his heart jumped, when a churning tide of water spilled halfway into the yard. The sea was already at the village!

Something had to be done. And fast. But what could he do? The only other people in the village at this time were those too old and frail to do anything. There were many like that in the village. Often, they were left with very young children. They could all be trapped and drowned if the sea continued to rise.

He tried to shout, but he could hardly hear his own voice! He stopped for a moment to think. There must be something useful that even he could do. But what was it? Perhaps Fusa was aware of what was going on in his mind. The dog had stopped whimpering and barking. Now it looked relaxed and there was a knowing and reassuring look in its eyes.

That was the moment Sosu got his idea. "The drums!" he said to himself, or perhaps to the dog, loudly. It meant getting out and trying to reach the drum shed behind the chief's house. With the swirls of frothy water everywhere, that could be dangerous even for a person with good legs.

But now, he could only think about the many young children, the sick and the very old people, and all the animals that were in serious danger. The look in Fusa's eyes did not only say it knew where to find the drums, it also said: "Don't be afraid. We will be all right!"

So with the dog leading the way, Sosu got out of the compound and on into the storm. The water reached to the heels of the dog and the screaming wind blew and tore at anything in its way.

But the dog would take several cautious steps ahead, stop, turn to look assuringly at its friend and wag its tail as if to say, "Come on. It's safe. Trust me. We can do it!"

Even today, Sosu does not know where the strength came from to strengthen his weak limbs, or the courage that drove him on. Somehow, he dragged himself along, leaning into the howling wind and sloshing through churning water!

Nothing happened to them and they reached the drum shed dripping wet, but safe. The shed was built on a raised platform, so it was dry inside and Fusa looked really pleased. But now as the dog stood and wagged its tail, Sosu was faced with a different problem. He had never played a real drum before and did not know how to make it talk.

Again, Fusa made the first move. As if to say, "There is no time," the dog stood up to its full height on its hind legs and scratched at a medium-size drum with its paws.

When the top of the drum tilted towards Sosu, he had to stop it from falling on top of him. After that, he took the two sticks in his hands. He struck the top of the drum with one stick, then the other. He played it slowly at first. But suddenly, the storm, the pounding waves of water, the young children, the sick, the old, the animals, the crashing fences and snapping trees, all came rushing to him like moving pictures.

So he struck the drum harder and faster until he heard it above the shrieks and howls of the wind:

belem-belen-belem! bembem-bembem-bem-bem!
belem-bembem-belem-bembem-belem-bem-bem!
bem-bem-belem! bem-bem-belem! bem-bem belem!

The drum was heard by those at the farthest end of the lagoon and by those working in the fields. They were aware of the storm, so they said, "The drumming is coming from our village. This is unusual. There must be trouble there. Let's go!"

It was heard by the people in the neighbouring village. They too said, "The drumming is from the village on the sandbar. They are in trouble. Let's go!"

So through the rain and storm, they all came rushing to the village.

And what a shock awaited them! Waves as high as roofs were pounding the village! Some compounds were so flooded that it took a number of strong men to reach them.

They worked hard, moving from compound to compound, as they searched for those who were trapped.

They said: "We were just in time, thanks to the drummer!"

"But who was the drummer?" somebody asked.

Suddenly, one of the men said loudly, "The boy who can't walk!"

"Oh, and his dog!" another added.

"But there was nobody in their house except the chickens in the rafters. The boy and the dog must be somewhere. Let's look for them."

The anxious men soon found them, thanks to Fusa's sharp ears and short excited barks.

"Here they are!" the men said. "The brave drummer and his friend! Well done! Well done!"

He was soon riding on strong shoulders, with Fusa leaping into the air to reach him.

That was the beginning. Everybody heard about him. The newspapers and people from the radio and TV came all the way to the village, just to see and talk to him! And of course, they took many pictures of him, his friend Fusa and his family.

He remembers being asked many questions, including why he did something so risky and silly. And when asked about what he would like the most, he remembers saying something about being able to walk and going to school.

In the weeks that followed, the broken houses and fences were all rebuilt and mended. Best of all, the one dusty, bumpy street of the village was scraped to make it even and smooth and it was extended right to the front gate of Sosu's house.

Then there was the big day at the village square. There was much singing, drumming and dancing. But suddenly it stopped and the chief stood up and spoke: "People of this good village, we are all here and happy today because of one brave little man – and his dog!"

Before he knew what was happening, Sosu was on shoulders again. Everything else that followed was like a dream. He was carried right across the square for people to see and cheer.

When the strong arms finally lowered him down, it was not onto the hard dusty ground. There was a gleaming, new wheelchair in front of him and that is where they put him.

Now, he too goes to school, pushed gladly in his wheelchair by the other children of the village. He is just one of the boys of the small village, somewhere between the sea and the lagoon.

The Little Blue Boy
by Fatou Keïta

Once upon a time in the pretty village of Koba, in the heart of Africa, there lived a young couple who were very much in love. But in spite of all the love they had for each other, they were not able to have a child. And yet this was their most cherished dream. They had been waiting for the happy event for a long time...

Finally, the young woman's tummy started to swell and there was joy in the little chilli-pepper-coloured hut. Papa Fanga and Mama Fanga made a thousand and one plans!

"This baby will be wonderful," they said.

"It'll be a handsome boy," said Papa Fanga. "He'll be big and strong. He'll have your lovely eyes, my beautiful one, and your dark ebony colour!"

"No, it'll be a lovely little girl with big, black eyes and fair skin like you," replied Mama Fanga, laughing.

And every day Mama Fanga's tummy got bigger and bigger. Soon she started feeling pains. Papa Fanga and Mama Fanga knew that at last the day they had been waiting for so long had come. They sent for old Mamata, the midwife.

The baby was finally about to be born and fill its parents with happiness. It would be just like any other baby but it would be extra special because it would be theirs.

The old midwife, with her expert hands, stayed alone with Mama Fanga in the little chilli-pepper-coloured hut. The whole family waited around the hut. Grandmothers, grandfathers, uncles, aunts, sisters, cousins…

Time passed, slowly, too slowly. Papa Fanga thought that this birth was taking too long!

Suddenly, after the long hours of waiting, they heard the first cries of the newborn baby. Phew! They started dancing around the hut, waiting to see it. They danced, and they danced!

But the door of the hut did not open. Old Mamata did not come out with the baby, as was the custom.

Little by little, the dancing stopped and a frosty silence came over the gathering.

Anxiety began to appear on the faces of the grown-ups. Yet everyone could hear the baby. It was crying so loudly! It must be very strong.

But Mamata still would not come out. Papa Fanga became so impatient that he decided to go and see what was happening in the little hut.

He opened the door, and there … goodness gracious! Mama Fanga was looking in wide-eyed disbelief at a beautiful baby … that was blue! It was a little boy, just like all other little boys except that this one was blue. A lovely bright blue from head to toe!

In all her time as a midwife, old Mamata had never seen anything like it! Yet she had seen so many babies, for she had helped deliver all the children in the village. She sat dumbfounded on a high stool staring at the little blue baby. She could not move an inch. All she could do was look at it, her eyes wide in amazement. Papa Fanga came closer. He picked up the little blue baby and gently held it against his chest.

Time went by. Little Blue Boy grew up. He was like all the other children his age – sometimes nice or naughty, mischievous, high spirited or even horrid… He was a joy to his parents, but this joy was tinged with a deep sadness. Why was he blue? Why?

To keep him out of sight, Papa Fanga had put up a huge fence around their hut. That way, Little Blue Boy could run and play without being the object of too much curiosity.

One day, when Papa Fanga was away and Mama Fanga was busy in the hut, Little Blue Boy opened the fence gate and ventured out.

Everything seemed so big, for he had been shut up all his life. Soon, attracted by a lot of shouting, he went straight to where a dozen children his age were playing.

"Little Blue Boy!" they shouted when they caught sight of him.

Of course they had all heard of this little blue boy but they had never set eyes on him. He had never seen them, either. They stared at one another for a long time. Then the children came a little closer to Little Blue Boy and touched him to see if his colour would stay on their fingers.

"Why are you blue?" asked one of them suddenly.

Little Blue Boy opened his eyes wide. He had never asked himself that question. Apart from the water he drank, everything he knew had a colour. The sky, the clouds, the animals, the trees, the flowers, everything!

"And you, why have you all got chocolate-coloured skin?"

"What colour skin?"

"Cho-co-late!" cried Little Blue Boy. Seeing the children's blank faces, he went on, "Yes, one day my uncle came back from a distant land where it's cold and he brought me a big box. Inside there were little squares of chocolate – you eat them, they're delicious. You can let them melt on your tongue or you can crunch them. Some of them are very dark, some are deep brown, others light brown and some are even white. They are lovely to look at, but the main thing is they're delicious. They're the same colour as you!"

The children looked at one another very closely for a while. Sure enough, none of them was quite the same colour as the other and there was even one that was an albino. But none of them was blue! And what were these little squares the same colour as them that you could eat?

"*We* are all normal," said Tchedjan, the biggest child. *You*, you're different. You're blue! So we're not playing with you."

"Why?" asked Little Blue Boy, surprised.

"Because you're blue," cried the children, who then ran off at top speed breaking out with peals of laughter.

Little Blue Boy went back home. But he was not sad. Quite the opposite! He was spellbound by what had happened and all excited.

The next day, Little Blue Boy slipped away from his parents again, and went back to where the children were.

"It's Little Blue Boy again!" they shouted, pointing at him.

Before they had time to do anything else, Little Blue Boy went up to a dog that one of them was holding.

"Why does your black dog have white spots?" he asked.

"Because!" replied little Bouba, shrugging his shoulders.

"It's normal," replied Tchedjan. "It's black and white, that's all! That's its normal colour."

"Why's that normal?" asked Little Blue Boy. "My dog is all white!"

The puzzled children looked at Bouba's dog as if they were seeing it for the very first time. It was quite true that it was black and white, but nobody had ever asked himself why! There was nothing out of the ordinary about this dog! Fancy asking such stupid questions! They burst out laughing and ran off.

Two days later, when they were playing with a bird they had just caught, they saw Little Blue Boy scampering happily towards them again.

"What a lovely bird," he said "Why is it red, blue, yellow and green? It's got four colours all to itself!"

Tchedjan angrily let go of the bird, which quickly flew away letting out a husky cry as if to thank Little Blue Boy.

"There," said Tchedjan, "no more bird, no more colours! No more stupid questions! Leave us alone!"

And he went off sniggering, followed by the other children. But lo and behold, a few moments later, Little Blue Boy was there again. This time he placed himself squarely in the middle of the group, and looked at them each in turn.

"You, why have you got white teeth?" he asked the one who was laughing stupidly. "And you," he said to the tallest one, "why have you got a big nose? And you, why is your tongue pink? You, why are your ears so small? And him, why is he white? Has he lost his colour?"

Little Blue Boy did not even pause to breathe. For several minutes he asked them all sorts of questions. Then, pleased with himself, he finally stopped.

"Well, are you going to answer me?' he said innocently.

"Er, um," the biggest one began. "Your questions are really too stupid!"

Clearly, Tchedjan was embarrassed. He could not answer this funny Little Blue Boy's questions. But as the leader of the group, he could not let himself look flustered. He was just about to open his mouth when Little Blue Boy took hold of his hands and asked him very seriously: "Why are the palms of your hands lighter than the rest of your body?"

Well, that was too much! Tchedjan tore his hands away from Little Blue Boy's and hid them behind his back. All the other children looked at their hands. It was true, yes, the palms of their hands were all lighter than the rest of their bodies. Why? How to answer that question?

"Come on," shouted Tchedjan to the others. "Let's go play without him."

They followed Tchedjan, but this time no one was laughing. They ran off quickly.

One of them, however, lingered behind the others and ended up coming back to Little Blue

Boy. His name was Nogoman, which means someone who enjoys eating.

"Do you want to play with me?" Little Blue Boy asked

"Yes," replied Nogoman straight away. The story of the little chocolate squares you could eat sounded particularly interesting!

"Can you show me what your chocolates are like? Just to look at."

"Of course, you can even taste them if you want!"

Nogoman's eyes lit up with expectation. And arm in arm they dashed off to Little Blue Boy's home. They went into the hut. Mama and Papa Fanga were out.

The little blue boy fetched his big box of chocolates, and opened it in front of Nogoman.

How pretty the chocolates were! They were exactly as Little Blue Boy had described them. They were all sorts of browns. They were exactly the same colour as the children in the village and, of course, their parents.

"Go ahead, have one," said Little Blue Boy. He swallowed a chocolate himself.

Nogoman chose a light-brown chocolate and slowly brought it to his mouth. Delicious! He had never tasted anything as sweet and good.

"Come on, let's play now," said Little Blue Boy.

But Nogoman wanted to go and tell the other children.

"I have to go home, but I'll come back tomorrow, I promise," he said and rushed off.

The next day Mama and Papa Fanga came home, and had a surprise. They heard the sound of children's laughter inside their hut. It was not mocking laughter, but joyful laughter. Who was there? They crept forward on tiptoe.

They saw a wonderful sight! There, in the middle of a group of boys and girls, sat their little blue son. He was telling all his new friends about his blue dreams. The children asked him questions, and his colour was not important any more.

From that day, Little Blue Boy became the friend of the village children. The chocolates quickly disappeared, but the children had learned not to avoid him. Although he was blue, the little boy was just like them. But he always did ask embarrassing questions!

One day, you may be lucky enough to pass through the village of Koba. You will certainly come across the blue boy, who is not so little any more. But you will probably be the only one to notice that he is blue!

Half a Day
by Naguib Mahfouz

I proceeded alongside my father, clutching his right hand, running to keep up with the long strides he was taking. All my clothes were new: the black shoes, the green school uniform and the red *tarboosh*. My delight in my new clothes, however, was not altogether unmarred, for this was no feast day but the day on which I was to be cast into school for the first time.

My mother stood at the window watching our progress, and I would turn towards her from time to time, as though appealing for help. We walked along a street lined with gardens; on both sides were extensive fields planted with crops, prickly pears, henna trees and a few date palms.

"Why school?" I challenged my father openly. "I shall never do anything to annoy you."

"I'm not punishing you," he said, laughing. "School is not a punishment. It is a factory that makes useful men out of boys. Don't you want to be like your father and brothers?"

I was not convinced. I did not believe there was really any good to be had in tearing me away from the intimacy of my home and throwing me into this building that stood at the end of the road like some huge, high-walled fortress, exceedingly stern and grim.

When we arrived at the gate we could see the courtyard, vast and crammed full of boys and girls. "Go in by yourself," said my father, "and join them. Put a smile on your face and be a good example to others."

I hesitated and clung to his hand, but he gently pushed me from him. "Be a man," he said. "Today you truly begin life. You will find me waiting for you when it's time to leave."

I took a few steps, then stopped and looked but saw nothing. Then the faces of boys and girls came into view. I did not know a single one of them, and none of them knew me. I felt I was a stranger who had lost his way. But glances of curiosity were directed towards me, and one boy approached and asked, "Who brought you?"

"My father," I whispered.

"My father's dead," he said quite simply.

I did not know what to say. The gate was closed, letting out a pitiable screech. Some of the children burst into tears. The bell rang. A lady came along,

94

followed by a group of men. The men began sorting us into ranks. We were formed into an intricate pattern in the great courtyard surrounded on three sides by high buildings of several floors; from each floor we were overlooked by a long balcony roofed in wood.

"This is your new home," said the woman. "Here too there are mothers and fathers. Here there is everything that is enjoyable and beneficial to knowledge and religion. Dry your tears and face life joyfully."

We submitted to the facts, and this submission brought a sort of contentment. Living beings were drawn to other living beings, and from the first moments my heart made friends with such boys as were to be my friends and fell in love with such girls as I was to be in love with, so that it seemed my misgivings had had no basis. I had never imagined that school would have this rich variety. We played all sorts of different games: swings, the vaulting horse, ball games. In the music room we chanted our first songs. We also had our first introduction to language. We saw a globe of the Earth, which revolved and showed the various continents and countries. We started learning the numbers. The story of the Creator of the universe was read to us, we were told of His present world and of His hereafter, and we heard examples of what He said. We ate delicious food, took a little nap and woke up to go on with friendship and love, play and learning.

As our path revealed itself to us, however, we did not find it as totally sweet and unclouded as we had presumed. Dust-laden winds and unexpected accidents came about suddenly, so we had to be watchful, at the ready and very patient. It was not all a matter of playing and fooling around. Rivalries could bring about pain and hatred or give rise to fighting. And while the lady would sometimes smile, she would often scowl and scold. Even more frequently she would resort to physical punishment.

In addition, the time for changing one's mind was over and gone and there was no question of ever returning to the paradise of home. Nothing lay ahead of us but exertion, struggle and perseverance. Those who were able, took advantage of the opportunities for success and happiness that presented themselves amid the worries.

The bell rang announcing the passing of the day and the end of work. The throngs of children rushed towards the gate, which was opened again. I bade farewell to friends and sweethearts and passed through the gate. I peered around but found no trace of my father, who had promised to be there. I stepped aside to wait. When I had waited a long time without avail, I decided to return home on my own. After I had taken a few steps, a middle-aged man passed by and I realised at once that I knew him. He came towards me, smiling, and shook me by the hand, saying, "It's a long time since we last met – how are you?"

With a nod of my head, I agreed with him and in turn asked, "And you, how are you?"

"As you can see, not all that good, Allah be praised!"

Again he shook me by the hand and went off. I proceeded a few steps, then came to a startled halt. Good Lord! Where was the street lined with gardens? Where had it disappeared to? When did all these vehicles invade it? And when did all these hordes of humanity come to rest upon its surface? How did these heaps of refuse come to cover its sides? And where were the fields that bordered it? High buildings had taken over, the streets surged with children and disturbing noises shook the air. At various points stood conjurors showing off their tricks and making snakes appear from baskets. Then there was a band announcing the opening of a circus, with clowns, and weightlifters walking in front. A line of trucks carrying central security troops crawled majestically by. The siren of a fire engine shrieked, and it was not clear how the vehicle would cleave its way to reach the blazing fire. A battle raged between a taxi driver and his passenger, while the passenger's wife called out for help and no one answered. Good God! I was in a daze. My head spun. I almost went crazy. How could all this have happened in half a day, between early morning and sunset? I would find the answer at home with my father. But where was my home? I could see only tall buildings and hordes of people. I hastened on to the crossroads between the gardens and Abu Khoda. I had to cross Abu Khoda to reach my house, but the stream of cars would not let up. The fire engine's siren was shrieking at full pitch as it moved at a snail's pace, and I said to myself, "Let the fire take its pleasure in what it consumes." Extremely irritated, I wondered when I would be able to cross. I stood there a long time, until the young lad employed at the ironing shop on the corner came up to me. He stretched out his arm and said gallantly:

"Grandpa, let me take you across."

Bulubulu and Bamboko
by Naiwu Osahon

My name is Lolobiri.

Every rat in the world is in my room right now, I tell you. They started arriving in trickles several Moons ago, setting up work camps in the remote regions of my room. First to make an appearance are the scouts; followed by their architects, engineers and building-site workers. Now they have assembled in my room, a gigantic complex of homes, community centres, hospitals, restaurants, shopping malls, laundries, toilets, the lot. The construction work never seems to end, but the big bosses have started to arrive at last. They have got to be the leaders because they are bigger and more arrogant. If it is not a conference they are setting up, then it must be some anniversary celebration or a weird festival of sorts. Whatever it is they are putting together could last forever because they have dug deep into my system and are boisterous and expansive about it in a settled kind of way.

The noise of the construction work is nothing now, compared with the cacophony of intimidating, frightening, whimpering, munching shrills, and they never seem to need a break. The younger ones are forever wrestling and shoving each other around, competing for space, food and toys.

If there is any rat anywhere in the world not attending this great gathering in my room right now, then the rat is either too sick or too old to travel. It is as serious as that. Fat rats, thin rats, pregnant rats, baby rats, every rat that is any rat in the rat world is here, I am sure of it. They have taken over my entire shadowed space with such daring, I have become a total jelly in their midst. A stranger in my own room. My relatives and I would be surprised if their agenda excludes determining what to do about my nuisance value.

I do not scare them. They actually stand up to me, on a one-on-one basis, when I challenge them. They parade leisurely in front of me, sometimes in tow, in their dark-grey, ever-shining, hairy frippery, as if in military formations. I have tried to lure them into the open space with the best food available to me, but they eat everything I offer and come back into the room giggling, whimpering and dancing as if to ask for more. Traps snap ceaselessly around the clock in my room disturbing my concentration, rest or sleep, but catching too few rats. They endlessly taunt me by cheekily displacing my carefully arranged decorative items around the room. They have learnt to dodge and steal baits from traps and are glowing and getting fat from eating the poison I spray on their paths.

All attempts at dislodging them from my room have failed. They don't appear to ever need rest or sleep. I can hardly ever surprise them. Most times I injure myself chasing after them. I still nurse a cut on my left toe from my most recent attempt to murder one of them with a machete. They are so nimble and agile; they virtually dissolve through solid brick walls when being pursued. I am already seriously considering abandoning my room to them. What else is there to do? My poverty has not discouraged them; rather it has toughened them to eat whatever they can get to survive. Wooden doors, rags, paintings, precious books, manuscripts, newspapers, magazines, buttons, paper bags, sand, rotten food, you name it, everything is food to these ghetto rats.

Why have the rats chosen our spiritless room as their residence, you might want to ask? I suggest you direct that question to the rats because if I knew the answer, I would have been rid of them by now. All I can tell you and this is in strict confidence, is that my room is in a derelict house in the heart of a Lagos shanty town called Mushin. The poorest people in the world live here so my lowly sanctuary is typical in my dilapidated neighbourhood. My co-tenants and neighbours probably have as many rats in their rooms as I have, but that is not really my business, is it? If they want to tell you about their worries, let them write their own books. I have enough problems of my own right now, as you can see.

The only modern thing in my room is a 20-year-old charcoal stove we use on the rare occasions that we have something to cook. Like the dirty stove, which despite regular scrubbing with sand, still looks like something rescued from a sewer, our room walls are peeling and are smeared with oil and grime of every conceivable nature. The walls have not smelt paint for the better part of 30 years at least.

The room has an invalid food cupboard that is held together with ropes and steadied with bricks. The cupboard was inherited from my grandfather, so now you know its age. They don't make cupboards like this any more. It is not that I am attached to it; I just don't have the money to replace it, that's all. Now the cupboard is the dream home of a mother rat and her husband.

I must tell you about this mother rat. We are

friends now, I think. I call her Pupu for no apparent reason. Don't ask me what she calls me. All I can tell you is that I broke one of her legs during a hot chase some while ago. I can't remember seeing her while she was recovering from her leg injury. Just as I was beginning to think I had succeeded in reducing my rat population by one, I saw her recently, waddling about pregnant with a broken hind leg. She is not scared of me at all now.

One early morning, during the recent Harmattan season, Pupu gave birth to a bunch of baby rats in a litter of waste paper and other junk in the deep recess of my disabled cupboard. The babies are all greyish in colour as usual, with tiny whiskers and hard, slim tails. The babies seem to have no care in the world, except to romp and roll over each other and their mother all day long.

Of the literally millions of rats in my room, Pupu and her family seem to have the most ideal home. The cupboard is only the entrance to their hole in the wall. The hole is dark, sandy, stony with waste paper and other junk for cushions. Besides, they have a monopoly on our food cupboard. Occasionally, the baby rats would kick the stones at each other as if in a football match and it does not matter whether they are hustling their mother or playing on their own, they make endless, joyous, sharp, hissing noises. Now and again one of them would stray from their mother to explore the surroundings and skitter back at the slightest sign of danger such as when any member of my household enters the room. The most restless of Pupu's kids and obviously the most troublesome, we call Bulu.

Bulubulu just would not stay in one place for any length of time. The mother would shout and shout at her to stay close. "Bulu, come back here at once," Pupu would shout, and Bulu would return reluctantly to the mother only to take off again moments later. One of her brothers, who is aggressive too, sometimes follows Bulu about to explore their surroundings. We call this one, Bamboko. By and large, Bamboko does not upset their mother half as much as Bulu does. "Where is Bulu again? Bulu, Buluooo," the mother would be heard shouting at the top of her voice and Bulu would answer from a distance. "Yes, mummy, I am coming, mummy," and yet, she would take a while to return to the safety of the family hideout. Pupu keeps warning Bulu that she would one day get lost or get killed by my wicked family and me. Bulu would sulk for a while, as if sorry for the nuisance she is creating, but moments later, she would forget everything the mother said and take off again. One evening Bulu disappeared again.

Pupu called and called but Bulu would not respond nor could she be found in all her usual play places Bamboko pointed out to Pupu's search party.

Bulu, unknown to her mother, was trapped in the boot of my junior brother's car. He had come to visit me that Saturday evening with his wife and two kids. Bulu playfully got into the boot through a tiny opening underneath the car but could not get back out. Not long after Bulu was trapped, the car revved and drove away.

Junior is doing very well for himself. He is an accountant in an oil company. He loved school as a young man and made the most of the opportunities he had to study. I did not. I dropped out halfway through secondary school and the difference in our lifestyles now shows up that early, costly mistake in my life. He is 34 years old and has two children, both boys. One is four and the other is two and a half years old. His wife, Kike, is 28 years old and a highly qualified lawyer. She works with a successful private firm of lawyers in Lagos. Junior and his family live in a posh duplex in an exclusive and affluent district of Lagos called Victoria Island.

Bulu had arrived at her new home. She found everything too outlandish, strange and difficult to adjust to initially, especially as she had to start fending for herself at such an early age. She had a whole big house to herself alone and food was in abundance. Butter, cakes, meat, you name it, were often being thrown away in large quantities under the pretext that they had gone bad.

Bulu, however, soon got used to the good life and even quickly began to develop a foreign accent judging by the sharpness in her squeak. Her grey skin had begun to glow like a mohair suit and she had an equally plush-looking boyfriend visiting regularly from a neighbouring duplex. They were still debating which of their two homes to adopt after marriage.

There wasn't much to choose between the two homes in terms of amenities. Also both families of the two duplexes had what the rats considered a sickening aversion to rats. The only difference was that Bulu's hosts fumigated their home with chemicals to kill rats, cockroaches and other insects once every six months, whereas the other family did theirs every three months. By the time Bulu was 18 months old, she had forgotten she ever had a difficult early three weeks in life. Bulu was looking very well kept, her personality elegant, robust and affluent from the rich grooming and good food she had become used to. She was still full of pranks though and on one Saturday evening while running around the house as usual, she saw food being loaded into the boot of Junior's car. More out of curiosity than need, she hid in the boot to snip at and waste some of the foodstuff. While in the boot, the car suddenly started moving. She could not see what was going on outside the boot but felt safe enough inside the boot anyway.

The car, some two hours later, came to a final halt. When the boot was opened for the food in it to be taken out, Bulu sneaked out and followed the food carriers into what she considered to be a terrible-looking, dirty, smelly kitchen. The small room was crammed with the legs of some ten or more people. There were legs everywhere and someone nearly stepped on Bulu, so she dodged and jumped into an ugly looking, half-opened cupboard to hide in.

Bamboko was the first to recognise Bulu in the safety of their hole behind the cupboard. "Am I seeing a ghost or what? Bulu, are you really here?" Bamboko screamed as he sprang to hug his long-lost sister robustly.

Bulu recognised Bamboko at once too and screamed: "My brother Bamboko!" with great joy.

Bamboko, still excited, started inviting everyone, including Bulu's other brothers and sisters, several wives, cousins, nephews and nieces to come and greet their long-lost relative. "We thought you were dead and now you have returned, looking so affluent and rich. I wish Mum could see you now," Bamboko said.

"Where is she, and Dad, too?" Bulu asked presently.

"They are both dead. The Lolobiris killed them both with their stupid traps, within weeks of each other, a few months ago," Bamboko said.

As a lavish welcome-home party started building up, Bulu told the story about the wonderful paradise for rats at the other end of town. She told them she had a state-of-the-art kitchen, all to herself and good quality food in abundance. Electricity and water were available all hours of the day at the push of a button. "I even have satellite dishes and numerous TVs to watch."

"What is TV?" one infant rat asked.

"Moving picture box," an elder rat responded.

"How can any rat live the way you are all living here, crowded in one small dark hole with hardly any food of value to eat? You don't have water, electricity, not even a comfortable bed to sleep in at night. There are too many mouths to share this squalid life. You can't keep eating trash and sleeping rough in dirty, unhealthy surroundings while a paradise for rats, called Victoria Island, is only a car ride away," Bulu said.

All the rats agreed that Bulu was making sense and that her prosperous look was sufficient proof of the wonderful place called Victoria Island.

"I have problems too," Bulu said, "but not about food or large, clean accommodation. I have too much of such things and no one to share them with. It is lonely out there but the real problem is the once-in-a-while chemical warfare against our hideouts. I have learnt to dodge this and survive and I think so can you. I would like to propose that you all move to Victoria Island with me," Bulu concluded.

Everyone shouted their approval and clapped heartily. Bamboko, who had become the father figure of the family since their parents died, cautioned that they had better not get carried away so easily. That the best thing to do was for some three or four of them to follow Bulu and check out the life she was talking about first before dislodging the entire family from Mushin.

Bamboko and three others, including a cousin about six months' old, a niece three months' old and a kid three and a half weeks' old went with Bulu to Victoria Island to spend a week. By the end of the second day, Bamboko was already complaining bitterly about life at Victoria Island. He and his team of visitors couldn't wait for Saturday evening to come when Junior was expected to make his regular visit to his brother's home at Mushin. There was a lot of food all right but it was too sweet and intoxicating. They were using too much wine and condiments for everything. There was too much leisure as well and it was creating serious boredom. All they had to do all day long was sleep, eat and sleep, and Bamboko and his team could not deal with such idleness.

Victoria Island was like a ghost town compared to the bustling Mushin metropolis. Families kept to themselves in their homes and hardly said hello to each other on the streets. You couldn't even giggle and romp all over the place for fear of disturbing neighbours with noise. Of course, there was plenty of accommodation space but it was as cold as a mortuary particularly at night because of air conditioners and so Bamboko soon caught pneumonia. But perhaps the most intolerable aspect of the visit to Victoria Island was the vicious chemical attack on their hideouts. The rats had to hide in almost totally sealed-up containers while the hostilities lasted. It was a horrible experience and they all nearly suffocated from it. Bamboko and the baby rat were still coughing seriously from the chemical attack two days later.

At the end of the week, a young rat was left to keep Bulu company and to help her colonise Victoria Island, while the rest of the Mushin clan happily returned to their ever bustling home.

Miss Johnson
by Véronique Tadjo

Miss Johnson is a young woman with a slender body and a serene look on her face. She usually goes unnoticed because shyness makes her stoop slightly. But her most striking feature is her mouth with its neatly lined bright teeth.

Every morning at seven o'clock sharp, she leaves the two-bedroom flat she shares with her younger sister and heads for the main junction that is busy with cars.

She lives in a crowded area of the capital, bustling with activity. The sound of honking mixed with the revving of engines and the shouts of taxi drivers advertising their destinations creates a terrible din, which mars the morning brightness of the sky.

If all goes well, that is if her bus is not late or if the traffic jam is not too big, Miss Johnson arrives at her office, a small room lost in the huge building of the Ministry of Social Affairs, at eight thirty.

As soon as she opens the door, she puts on the fan (the air conditioning doesn't work any longer), takes several thick, dog-eared files out of a drawer and starts writing in her small and careful hand.

The files all look the same. She copies down names, addresses, dates and puts numbers in a register. She does this mechanically, raising her head from time to time to talk to her colleagues, who arrive much later. She is always the first one in and the last one out.

She is bored, though. This routine work weighs down on her mind and makes her feel morose. Days seem endless, each hour stretching to infinity. Luckily, from time to time she has to take an urgent file to the other wing of the building. It breaks the great monotony of her time a bit.

Around midday, a young girl comes in without knocking. She carries a tray of oranges on her head. She puts it down on a chair and hands two already-peeled fruits to Miss Johnson. They smile at each other. Miss Johnson is her best customer.

Later on, when the working day is over, after the boss has called her several times to his office to give her more files, Miss Johnson will go back home.

She will follow the same route: first, coming down the long staircase because the elevator is always out of order, then along the crowded street that leads her to the bus stop surrounded by queues of vehicles that are overloaded and noisy. She will wait until her bus arrives at last. A stampede starts in order to get a seat inside.

When Miss Johnson reaches her area, she will walk looking straight ahead, with one thing on her mind: to get home as quickly as she can.

But this particular afternoon, her attention is caught by a small shop that has just opened. No, to be more precise, it isn't just any shop, it is a workshop. A big sign reads: PAINTER.

Miss Johnson comes closer and looks inside through a half-open window.

There is nobody in the workshop but she can see paintings hanging from all the walls. Some more are stacked up on a small table. She is dazzled. She has never seen anything like this! All this beauty found in one place touches her heart. She feels like she has discovered a treasure island.

She wonders who the artist is and how he got the idea to open a workshop in such a noisy, crowded area; a place where everybody always seems in a hurry, preoccupied by the hardship of the city.

She is thinking about all this, squinting to take in more of the workshop where obscurity is gradually setting in.

And it is love at first sight! The paintings make her feel dizzy. Her heart beats fast. When her fingers gripping the side of the windowsill start feeling numb, she realises that she has been standing there, admiring the paintings for too long.

Evening is falling. Miss Johnson comes out of her dream and resumes her walk.

At home, she still feels excited about her discovery. She talks passionately about it to her sister who listens, perplexed. It is the first time her sister has heard her speak so enthusiastically about something.

Miss Johnson has a light dinner and afterwards decides to retire early to bed. The television programmes don't interest her.

However, once in bed, she can't fall asleep. The memory of all those paintings keeps coming back to her.

When, in the end, she drifts off, she dreams about them. She sees herself hanging one of these paintings in her flat. She imagines how transformed her life would be, monotony leaving her to be replaced by beauty.

The next morning, as soon as she wakes up, Miss Johnson makes up her mind to go back to the workshop.

She takes her breakfast in a hurry and goes out. She arrives at the workshop, to find the artist already at work. He is busy painting a big canvas. So much of his attention goes into it, he doesn't even see that Miss Johnson is looking at him intently.

He is an artist who lives in a simple way. He is wearing a very ordinary shirt and a pair of trousers covered with stains from the paint. On his feet are sandals.

When the young man notices her at last, he gives her a warm welcome. Then they start chatting. Miss Johnson tells him about her admiration for his work. He, in turn, explains the symbols in his paintings.

After their first meeting, Miss Johnson visits his workshop every day to watch him paint. Each morning, before going to the office, she brings him some food, dishes that she has prepared the night before. She knows that he doesn't eat enough and that he would stay hungry for the whole day if she did not take care of him.

On her way home, Miss Johnson comes round again to collect the plates and follow the progression of the big painting he is working on. There are more and more colours, while shapes emerge and lines impose themselves. She stays there, rooted, watching him work, fascinated by the unfolding process, fascinated by the mystery of creation.

Then, one day, the painting is finished. It is there, in front of them, in all its perfection. The artist smiles at Miss Johnson, an air of great satisfaction in his eyes. She shares his happiness at having completed his work, at last.

But how surprised she is when the young man takes the painting with both hands and gives it to her saying: "Here, it is for you!"

Miss Johnson can't believe her luck. She is overjoyed and her heart is filled with gratitude and feelings of friendship.

She can't stop admiring the painting which now adorns her flat. The more she looks at it, the more it makes her dream. A new world opens up to her.

She wants to meet people. She wants to make new friends. She is like a child who is eager to share her joy, to shout it on the rooftops so everybody can hear it.

Soon, Miss Johnson starts receiving visitors. People come to chat with her, have a drink and admire the painting. She talks about her friend, the artist, and they all want to see his workshop.

Joy enters the flat. Laughter is heard. Beauty settles.

Miss Johnson doesn't know what the future holds for her. She has no idea what her life will become. But one thing is for certain: she will always remember the afternoon when she discovered the paintings. The sun was descending on the city in a burst of fireworks.

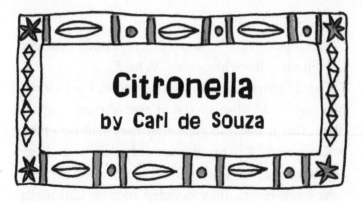

Citronella
by Carl de Souza

Once upon a time there lived a little girl called Citronella who would not hear.

She would hear neither the important things Yapana-Daddy told her.

Nor good advice from Mama-Mootye.

Nor the babble from her brothers and sisters.

"This child must be deaf," said Aunty Balsamine, who was always right. "If one can't hear, one is deaf." Everyone agreed. They decided that Citronella should see the local doctor. They called him Chicken-Doc, as he wasn't a very good doctor, but he was the only one around.

"Can you hear me?" asked Chicken-Doc while he examined her.

"What?" said Citronella.

"She's deaf," he confirmed.

Chicken-Doc prescribed drops of Uncorkol to clear her ears and pills of Volumax to take before meals. "This little girl should hear better, with this medicine, he said.

"Yes, yes, yes!" shouted everybody except Citronella who whispered: "What?"

The Uncorkol eardrops trickled-tickled down her ears and Volumax tasted worse than a bitter plant. But it became clear that they had no effect whatsoever: Citronella would still not hear anything she was told.

As a last resort, they decided to take Citronella to Mighty-Healer-Bilimbi whose magical powers were feared by everyone.

"Somebody has cast a spell upon this child," he declared as soon as he saw Citronella. "She can't hear because bad spirits are eating up the sounds before they reach her. You must grind up the shells of some big creepy-crawly-snails and sprinkle the powder on her head. Then paint her nose with the droppings of the bulbul bird," he said.

"Oh, I almost forgot. She should also hold a lighted red candle," he added.

Bilimbi's orders were promptly executed. They powdered her hair with ground-up shells of some big snails, smeared her nose with – yuck! – fresh bulbul droppings. She sat there, patiently, with a lighted red candle in her hand.

Then they asked her loudly: "Citronella, Citronella, can you hear us, now?"

"What?" said Citronella.

As she still would not hear after all that had been done, they no longer bothered with Citronella.

They left her with her Grandpa-Tambalakok, who was very, very old and who had been unable to hear anything for a long time. Grandpa-Tambalakok sat quietly in his armchair saying nothing. Not a single word. He just looked at Citronella, without blinking. Deep into her eyes. Finally, he struggled to his feet, took Citronella's hand and they left the house together.

They took a path that went through a hole in the hedge, leading to a sugar-cane field. A vast sugar-cane field freshly harvested, full of wind, light and sweet smells. They wandered along the furrows.

Little Citronella could feel the straw brush-sh-sh against her ankles, and the soil crunch-ch-ch under her feet. The breeee-zzzzzzz-e in her hair and the wwwwarmth of the sss-sun on her ch-ch-cheeeeeks. She saw the clouds fffff-leee in the sky, and the birds dance in the thorn bushes.

Grandpa-Tambalakok and Citronella found their way, slowly, towards the beach, guided by the rustling of the wings of the dragonflies and the flapping of the palm leaves in the wind. Waves lapped gently on the shore.

There, at last, they stopped, staring at the ocean

with the sound of their own breathing in their ears, their eyes full of mist and white birds.

Darkness came. Grandpa-Tambalakok, seated against the rocks, rested while Citronella, her head laid against his chest, listened to the beat of his old heart: "*Togodok-togodok-togodok.*"

They were found the next morning after a long night's search.

Grandpa-Tambalakok's eyes were closed. Citronella, who was sitting beside him, saw Yapana-Daddy and Mama-Mootye and Aunty Balsamine and her brothers and sisters and Chicken-Doc and Mighty-Healer-Bilimbi and many others running towards them.

"There they are! We've found them, Citronella and old Tambalakok!" they shouted.

Citronella jumped up and stood across their way, red with anger. She put her finger to her lips and said, "Shhhhh!" pointing at the sleeping man.

The shouts and cries and all the noise stopped abruptly. The whole crowd hushed to avoid waking up old Tambalakok.

For the first time, the people could hear the babbling of the water, the song of the wind in the casuarinas, and the clicking of the crabs' claws. They stood still and looked at Citronella, biting their lips, sorry for the way they had treated her.

For a long time, they stood there, together, near

Citronella and Tambalakok, listening. As they had never listened until then. To things you could not hear with your ears…

Tambalakok, the old man, never woke up. They dug a big bed for him in the fine beach sand so that he would never be far from the songs of the fish. They left him there to rest in peace.

Citronella returned home with the others. She carried the "*togodok*" of her grandpa's heart in her head, a "*togodok*" that, during the night, had hopped from Tambalakok's chest to nest in Citronella's head. She knew that, as long as she would hear this "*togodok*" sound, nobody could harm her. And that Yapana-Daddy, Mama-Mootye, the others, and herself, Citronella, would understand each other.

Father, Who Are You?

by Karen Press

Everyone was getting ready for the day when Father would come home from the mines. Mother scrubbed the walls and floor of the house, and hung up the bright red-and-black clothes that she kept for special days. Grandmother was weaving a new mat of dried grass to place on the floor where Father would sit. Kwezi, who was nine years old, swept the yard, and brushed the long hair of the goat until it was smooth and shining.

Only Boniswa had nothing to do. She was four years old. "You are too little to help us," said Kwezi. "Only big children like me know how to work in the house."

Boniswa wanted to cry. She felt a big tear start to run out of one eye. Mother saw the tear, and she kissed Boniswa on top of the head. "Why don't you go and see if the hen has laid any eggs?" she said. "That would be very helpful."

Boniswa went to the corner of the yard where the hen lived with her chickens. She looked in the pile of straw, but there were no eggs there. "Maybe the hen is still going to lay her eggs," she thought. "I will go for a walk, and look again when I come back."

She went out of the yard into the dusty field that stretched all the way to the top of the hill. There was nothing growing in the field. There had been no rain for many months, and all the mielies and pumpkins and tomatoes which mother had planted, had died before they were ripe.

This year, all the fields around the village were dry and empty. People said they had never had to wait so long for rain before. They were worried that no mielies or vegetables would grow, and they would go hungry.

On the edge of the field there was only one tiny plant growing. It was a bright-orange flower with dark-green leaves. Somehow it had stayed alive all these months without rain. Boniswa often came to visit the flower; she felt that it was her own special part of the field. Now she sat down next to it and thought about Father.

He had been away a long time, almost a year. What did he look like? She could hardly remember. Tall, with big hands that felt rough like a stone, and a deep voice like thunder behind the hills – was that him? She wondered what he would say to her when he came home. Would he be cross with her like Kwezi, because she was too small to help with the housework? Or would he be kind, like Mother? She was a little bit frightened. "What if he doesn't like me?" she said to herself. "Maybe he won't remember who I am." This thought made her very sad. To stop herself from crying, she jumped up and ran back to look in the hen's straw for eggs. There was one egg there, and she picked it up and took it back to the house. "You will have to lay more eggs than this when Father comes," she said to the hen.

On the day that the bus arrived at the village from the mines, Kwezi and Boniswa went to meet Father.

There were many other children there, all waiting to greet their fathers. At last the bus arrived. It was covered in dust, from the long road through the hills. The men who climbed off all looked tired, as if they'd been travelling for many days. They carried suitcases and shopping bags full of clothes and food that they had brought from the city for their families.

"Where is Father?" Boniswa asked Kwezi.

"Shh!" was his answer. "Wait!" He sounded worried. Boniswa looked at him fearfully. Maybe he didn't remember Father, either? But just then he shouted, "There he is!" and ran towards the bus. Boniswa followed him. He stopped in front of a tall man who was wearing a grey jacket and brown cap.

"Father," he said, "it is me, Kwezi! And here is Boniswa!"

The man turned around, and when he saw the children a big smile spread across his tired face.

"Ah, my children!" he said. "It is very good to see you again!"

He held out his arms, and folded both children in a hug against his chest. Then he picked up his suitcase, and together the three of them walked towards the road that would take them back to the house, where Mother and Grandmother were waiting for them.

Along the way, Kwezi told Father all the things that had happened in the village during the past year, and Father asked him many questions about the house and the field.

Boniswa walked a little way behind them. "So this is Father," she thought. "He is bigger than I remembered, and his voice is deeper. I hope he does not ask me questions, the way he is doing with Kwezi. He will not like me if I cannot tell him clever things, like Kwezi can."

At home everything seemed different, now that Father was there. The house felt smaller, and at night when they all sat around the fire eating their supper, the shadows on the wall seemed much bigger than before. Instead of playing noisily around the house all day, the children sat quietly in the yard, so as not to disturb Father and the men from the village who came to visit him.

They talked for many hours about the fields where nothing would grow, and they argued about when the rain would come.

Boniswa was very shy in front of Father, and whenever he spoke to her she ran to stand next to Mother or Grandmother. Then Father's eyes grew sad, and he turned away with a sigh.

Sometimes Mother got cross with her. "Why do you run away from your father? she said. "That is a bad thing to do. You must show that you love him and respect him."

But Grandmother would answer her, "Leave the child alone. You cannot blame her. Her father is like a stranger to her. When she knows him better, she will not be frightened of him."

"Ah, but how long will there be, for her to learn to know him?" said her mother. "He must go away soon, back to the mines."

"Yes, it's a sad time that we're living in," said Grandmother. "Children are like strangers to their fathers. That is not good. It hurts the children, and the fathers."

Boniswa did not understand what they were saying but she knew that soon Father would have to leave them, to go back to the mine in the big city where he worked all year. She knew that she should feel very sad about this, but in a corner of her heart she couldn't help feeling happy. For once Father left, everything at home would be as it was before, and she would not have to be afraid of seeming stupid when he spoke to her, or of disturbing him in the house.

Whenever she could, she went to sit in the field next to her orange flower. Here she felt happy and free, watching the clouds make shapes in the sky, and listening to the wind blow through the grass.

But one day she saw that the flower was dying. Its leaves were turning brown, and the orange petals were curled back, ready to fall off. It could not live any longer without rain. Boniswa began to cry as she thought that soon her beautiful friend would disappear forever.

Just then a shadow fell over the flower. When she looked up, Boniswa saw Father standing there, looking down at her.

"Why are you crying, my daughter?" he asked.

Boniswa pointed at the flower. "My flower is dying," she said.

"Yes," said Father. "Poor flower. It cannot live without rain. But look – I will show you

134

something." Then he knelt down on the ground beside her, and with his long fingers he gently felt the dark place at the centre of the flower. He held out his hand to Boniswa. In the palm was a little pile of black things, like grains of sand.

"What are those?" asked Boniswa.

"They are seeds," said Father. This flower will die soon. But when the rains come, you can plant these seeds in the ground, and from each of them you will get a new flower, just as beautiful as this one."

"Truly, Father?" said Boniswa. "But when? When will the new flowers come?"

"Truly, my child," said Father. "The rains will come soon, maybe a month after I am gone from here. If you plant the seeds then, they will grow quickly, and before I come home again your new flowers will be ready."

"Will they still be here when you come again?" said Boniswa.

"I hope so," said Father. "If you look after them well, they will wait for me to return."

Then he got up from the ground. "Come," he said. "Let us go back to the house and find a safe place to keep these seeds, until the rains come." He took Boniswa by the hand, and together they walked home.

Now Boniswa was not frightened of Father any more, and she made him tell her every day how the seeds would turn into beautiful flowers.

When he had to leave again for the mines, everyone was very sad. Boniswa cried and cried as she watched him pack his suitcase. Before he left the house, he took her hand and went to stand in front of the little pot where they had placed the seeds.

"Do not be sad," he said to her. "While I am gone you must look after these seeds, and the plants that grow from them. Whenever you look at them, remember me, and know that as the plants grow taller, the time will get shorter until I come home again." Then he kissed her goodbye, and set out on the road to the village, where the bus was waiting to take him back to the city.

The rains came at last, and while everyone was planting vegetables in the fields, Boniswa took her pile of seeds out to the place where the orange flower had been, and planted them carefully in a row. Every day she went out to look after them, and to make sure that no insect harmed the little green shoots that soon appeared above the ground.

"Why do you go to the field all the time?" grumbled Kwezi. "You should stay here and help with the housework."

"I am helping." said Boniswa proudly. "I am looking after the flowers so that they will be ready for Father when he comes home."

About the Authors

Chinua Achebe is well known for his novels describing the effects of Western culture on traditional African society. Achebe has created his own style of writing, full of African imagery, cultural references and proverbs. His novels have been read by millions and been translated into numerous languages. He is one of the first African writers to also write for young people. He now teaches in the United States.

Born in Ghana, **Meshack Asare** studied Fine Art in his country and later taught for 12 years. He quickly developed a passion for writing and illustrating books for young people. His first picture book was published in 1970, and since then he has received many awards for his work.

In his writing, **Kariuki Gakuo** likes to combine his knowledge of ancient legends with a modern, creative style. He knows how to use the natural and supernatural features of East Africa in his narration to create a fascinating atmosphere.

Professor P Gurrey received a PhD from London University. In the 1940s he was a lecturer in English at the University College of the Gold Coast (Ghana). He has published educational material for teaching English in African schools.

Born and raised in Côte d'Ivoire, **Fatou Keïta** is now a lecturer at the English department of the University of Abidjan. She has been writing books for children for over a decade and is passionate about it. Her award-winning stories deal with a wide range of topics and are greatly enjoyed by her young readers.

Raised in a nomadic Maasai village in the north of Kenya, **Joseph Lemasolai Lekuton** was the only child in his family to go to school. He then went on to study in the United Sates in his late teens and now teaches history in Virginia. He has remained in touch with his roots and is very involved in community development projects in Kenya. 'A Lion Hunt' is based on memories of his childhood.

Born in Cairo, **Naguib Mahfouz** studied

philosophy at the University. He began writing at the age of 17. His first novel was published in 1939 and he has now written more than 40 books and countless short stories. He is famous for his description of Egyptian urban life and is considered to be the pioneer of modern fiction in Arabic. His style is poetic and full of symbolism. He was awarded the Nobel Prize for Literature in 1988.

Naiwu Osahon is a Nigerian writer living in Lagos. His inspiration often comes from oral traditions and his books have a strong message. His great sense of humour and his innovative writing style have assured him of a good readership. He is a strong believer in Pan Africanism, a political movement which aims to unify the whole of Africa.

A teacher of mathematics and English by training **Karen Press** is of South African origin. She is well known for her commitment to many educational projects directed at underprivileged children. She has done several workshops to stimulate budding authors and has also produced a film script and stories for newly literate adults. In 1987 she co-founded the publishing collective Buchu Books.

A writer, poet and philosopher, **Léopold Sédar Senghor** from Senegal was one of the founders of the Négritude movement in the 1940s. Together with other writers from Africa and the French West Indies, he formed a group who believed that literature could help free Africans from colonisation. When Senegal became independent in 1960, Senghor was elected president and managed to balance his political career with his writing.

Born in Rose-Hill, Mauritius, **Carl de Souza** studied Biology at the University of London and later became a teacher for several years. In 1995 he became the headmaster of St Mary's College in Rose-Hill. He writes regularly in reviews and literary magazines. He has also published three novels. 'Citronella' was his first story for young people but he now writes regularly for this age group. A multi-lingual writer, he is very rooted in the rich cultures of his island. His writing is full of references to Mauritius.

Véronique Tadjo is a writer, painter and illustrator from Côte d'Ivoire. She earned a BA in English from the University of Abidjan and a doctorate from the Sorbonne, Paris, in African American literature and civilisation. In 1983, she went to Howard University in Washington D.C. and subsequently became a lecturer at the University of Abidjan until she took up writing full time. Her work includes several collections of poems and novels. She illustrates the books she writes for children.

Acknowledgements

For permission to reproduce the following copyright material, the publisher thanks:

Léopold Sédar Senghor, 'Leuk-the-Hare Discovers Man', *La Belle Histoire de Leuk-Le-Lièvre*, Classiques Hachette, Paris, 1953. Translated into English by Véronique Tadjo.

'A Lion Hunt', *Facing the Lion: Growing Up Maasai on the African Savanna* by Joseph Lemasolai Lekuton and Herman Viola. Copyright © 2003. Reprinted with permission of National Geographic Books.

Meshack Asare, *Sosu's Call*, Sub-Saharan Publishers, Legon, Accra, Ghana, 1997.

Fatou Keita, 'The Little Blue Boy', Nouvelles Editions ivoiriennes, Abidjan, 1997.

'Half a Day', translated by Denys Johnson-Davis, copyright © 1991 American University in Cairo Press, from *The Time and the Place and Other Stories* by Naguib Mahfouz. Used by permission of Doubleday, a division of Random House Inc.

Véronique Tadjo, 'Miss Johnson', *La Chanson de la Vie*, Hatier-Ceda, Monde Noir Poche, Paris/Abidjan, 1989. Translated into English by the author.

Carl de Souza, 'Citronella', translated into English by the author.

Karen Press, 'Father, Who Are You?', *Children of Africa*, Buchu Books, Cape Town, 1987.

Every effort has been made to trace the copyright holders. The publishers would like to hear from any copyright holders not acknowledged.